Alex the Great

H. C. Witwer

Illustrated by Arthur William Brown

Along he comes with some dame he must have kidnapped from the Follies when Ziegfeld was busy countin' up the receipts or somethin'.

ALEX THE GREAT

BY

H. C. WITWER

Author of "From Baseball to Boches,"
"A Smile a Minute," etc.

ILLUSTRATED BY
ARTHUR WILLIAM BROWN

1919

DEDICATED TO
RALPH T. HALE
—EDITOR OF SMALL, MAYNARD AND COMPANY—
MY PUBLISHER—BUT STILL MY FRIEND

CONTENTS

ILLUSTRATIONS

Along he comes with some dame he must have kidnapped from the Follies when Ziegfeld was busy countin' up the receipts or somethin'. . . . . . . *Frontispiece*

I struck a match and he tells me they is 9,765,543 of them used in New York every fiscal year.

"She's going to marry me, she's going to marry me!"

She's knittin' a sweater for me that will prob'ly make me off her for life.

"How perfectly sweet! If you two only knew what a pretty picture you make!"

"Heavens!" says the vampire. "You must have worked all your life to acquire ignorance, for no one was ever born as stupid as you!"

When the dames cast languishing glances at his handsome form, he glared at them like an infuriated turtle.

CHAPTER I

INTRODUCING ALEX THE GREAT

Girls, listen—if friend hubby comes home to-night and while hurlin' the cat off his favorite chair, remarks that he's got a scheme to make gold out of mud or pennant winners out of the St. Looey Cardinals, don't threaten to leave him flat and accuse him of givin' aid and comfort to the breweries. Turn the gas out under the steak, be seated and register attention—because maybe he *has*!

Scattered around all the department stores, coal mines, butcher shops, the police force and banks, there's guys which can sing as well as Caruso, lead a band better than Sousa, stand Dempsey on his ear, show Rockefeller how to make money or teach Chaplin some new falls. Yet these birds go through life on eighteen dollars every Saturday with prospects, and never get their names in the papers unless they get caught in a trolley smash-up. They're like a guy with the ice cream concession at the North Pole. They got the goods, but what of it? As far as the universe is concerned it's a secret—they're there with chimes on, but nobody knows it but them!

Y'know this stuff about us all bein' neck and neck when we hit the nursery may be true, but, believe me, some guys are born to run second! They get off on the wrong foot, trailin' the leaders until the undertaker stops the race. They plod through life takin' orders from guys that don't know half as much about any given thing as they do; they never get a crack at the big job or the big money, although accordin' to Hoyle they got everything that's needed for both. Take Joey Green who used to be so stupid at dear old college that the faculty once considered givin' him education by injectin' it into his dome with a hypodermic. At forty he comes back to the campus to make 'em a present of a few new buildin's out of last month's winnin's from the cruel world. Where is Elbert Huntington, which copped all the diplomas, did algebra by ear and was give medals for out-brainin' the class? Where is *he*, teacher? And the echo chirps,

1

"Workin' for Joey Green, drawin' twenty a week and on the payroll as No. 543!"

The answer to this little thumb sketch is easy. Elbert Huntington had brains and Joey Green had confidence. Elbert *expected* to dumfound the world with what he knew, and Joey *did* dumfound it with what he didn't. Now if Joseph made good with nothin' but nerve, what could a guy do that had brains and nerve both?

I'll tell you.

After we won the world's series in 1914 and the dough had been divided up to the satisfaction of everybody but the guys that was in on the split, me and the wife had figured on one of them trips to Europe. You prob'bly know the kind I mean, "$900 and up. Bus to hotel on fifth morning out included." I had looked forward to this here expedition for thirty years, like a guy looks forward to eight o'clock the night he's gonna call on his first girl. We had learned French and Eytalian off of a phonograph record and from givin' them spaghetti dives a play. Also, I had collected a trousseau that would of made John Drew take arsenic if he'd ever of flashed me when I was dolled up for the street.

Prob'ly you have seen somethin' in the papers about how the old country was closed to traffic right then. From what I hear it was all dug up like lower Broadway and tourists had to detour by way of So. America, so we never got nearer Europe than the Williamsburg Bridge, and you can't see a thing from there.

Well, when we found out that as far as trips to Europe was concerned they was nothin' stirrin', the wife took both bank books and went down to Lakewood, while I stayed in New York as a deposit on the new flat. I went to the station with her and I'll betcha from the fond farewells we give each other, people must of thought she was gonna take the veil or somethin', instead of just goin' to entomb herself in Jersey for a month. I swore I'd be in every night at ten, although that's kinda late to start out for the night, and she promised not to get in no bridge mêlées where the sum they battled for was over six bits. Then we took some more bows on the lovin' good-by stuff, and I'm alone in the big city.

I managed somehow to live through the day, but the next afternoon I lured a bunch up to the flat for a little pinochle. I begin by invitin' two guys, but by the time we got to Harlem we was a dozen strong. Once inside the portals, it turns out that only six of them is wild about pinochle, so the rest of 'em take up the rugs, start the victrola and give themselves up to dancin'. Pretty soon the telephone rings with great violence. I grabbed the receiver and learned it was the woman which lives underneath.

"Them steamfitters you got rehearsin' up there has got to call it a day!" she says. "Otherwise I'll moan to the landlord. The chandelier has left the ceilin' already and four pieces of my chocolate set is busted. I never heard tell of such carryin' on!"

"Wait till you been here a little longer," I says, "I ain't carryin' on, me and some boy friends of mine is tryin' to kill a dull afternoon and —"

"If them's friends makin' that racket," she butts in, "I hope I have moved when your enemies call! What am I gonna do about that chocolate set, hey? D'ye hear — there goes another piece!"

"If I was in your place," I tells her, "I'd drink coffee, and if your furnishings is all as frail as that chocolate set you're featurin', you better grab hold of the piano, because I'm gonna sneeze!"

"Don't you dare make no cracks about my furniture!" she yells. "I got my opinion of what you do for a livin' when you can afford to be home in the daytime!"

"I make chocolate sets," I says. "We're workin' on one now and —"

"Wait till my husband comes home!" she cuts in. "He'll take care of you!"

"I don't need nobody to take care of me," I comes back, "I'm self supportin'."

"Why don't you let go there?" yells Eddie Brannan. "Are you and that dame doin' an act or what?"

Zip! she hangs up and just then the front door-bell makes good.

"See who it is!" I calls to one of the gang, sittin' in the game again. "Tell 'em I'm in Brazil and—"

Oh, boy!

One of them dead silences took place in the hall and—in walks the wife!

For the next five seconds it was so quiet in that flat that a graveyard would seem like a locomotive works alongside of it. Joe Leity starts to whistle soft and low, Abe Katz opens the dumbwaiter and looks down to see what kind of a jump it is and I dropped a hundred aces on the floor. The rest of the gang eases over to the door.

"Why—ah—eh—ah, what does this mean?" I says kinda weak. "I thought you had went to Lakewood."

"Well," she says, turnin' the eyes, that used to fill the Winter Garden every night, on the gang, "where d'ye figure I am now? I'll give you three guesses!"

"Ahem!" says Joe Leity, "I guess I'll blow! I—"

"Me, too!" pipes the gang like a chorus and does a few more vamps to the door.

"Why don't you introduce your friends?" says the wife. "Or maybe you just run across these boys yourself when you come in, heh?"

"Excuse!" I says. "This here's Joe Leity, Abe Katz, Phil Young, Red Dailey, Steve—"

"Never mind callin' the roll," she butts in. "I'll let it go en masse. I'm delighted to meet you all, and I hope you won't run away simply because I'm here."

"Oh, no—not at all—we ain't runnin' away!" they says.

"There's no reason for you boys *runnin'* anyways," the wife goes on, "because the elevator is right outside now and I think the boy is holdin' the car for you—"

They blowed!

"And now," says the wife to me, "what d'ye mean by bringin' them plumbers up here for a union meetin', eh?"

"Don't be always knockin'!" I answers, gettin' peeved. "Them boys is all honest and true, even if they do look a little rough to the naked eye. But how is it you come back to-day when you wasn't due for a month?"

"You're tickled to death to see me, ain't you?" she asks, pullin' the pout that formerly helped sell the magazines.

To be level with you, I was—mad and all.

"Why, dearie!" I remarks, kissin' her. "You know I—"

"Easy with the oil!" she cuts me off. "Get on your hat and coat; we're goin' right down to Grand Central Station."

"Don't you think it's liable to tire you, honey," I asks her, "runnin' back and forth from Lakewood like this?"

"I'm not goin' to Lakewood, Stupid," she says. "We're goin' down to meet Alex Hanley—of course you remember him?"

I threw in the self-starter on the old brain, but there was nothin' doin'.

"No!" I says. "To come right out with it—I don't. I realize though that he must be a lu-lu when we're goin' down and meet him at the station. What did he do—lick Dempsey?"

"Idiot!" says the wife, callin' me by her favorite pet name. "He's my cousin."

Oh, boy!

We was goin' down in the elevator and I sunk in the seat with a low moan. In the short space since me and the wife had been wed, I had met her father, six brothers, four nephews, three cousins and a bevy of her uncles. They all claimed they was pleased to meet me, though they couldn't figure how their favorite female relative come to fall for me—and then they folleyed that lead up with a request for everything from a job to ten bucks.

"All right, dearie," I says, finally, "I'm game! Believe me, though, while your family is all aces to me on account of bein' related to you, I often find myself wishin' that you had been an orphan!"

"I could of married a couple of millionaires!" sighs the wife. "And to think I turned 'em down for you!"

"If you had married a *couple* of millionaires, you would of been pinched!" I says. "What d'ye think this cousin of yours will want to start off with, from your affectionate husband?"

"Nothin'!" she tells me. "Alex never asked a favor in his life. Believe me, this one is different!"

"I can see that from here!" I says. "If you claim he won't take me for something he's different, all right. In fact I can hardly believe he belongs to the family at all."

6

"I was brought up never to brawl in the open," says the wife, "so I'm lettin' your insults go. This boy is fresh from the mountains of Vermont. He's never been to New York in his life and he's comin' here now to make his mark."

"I'll lay you eight to five I'm the mark!" I says.

We was at the station then, so we had to practise self-denial and quit scrappin'. The wife explained that she had hardly got to Lakewood when she found a telegram there from her cousin Alex sayin' that he was comin' down for a visit. So she beat it right back to meet him, not wantin' the poor kid to breeze into a town like New York, all by his lonesome.

Well, we stand in the middle of the waitin'-room like a couple of boobs for a while, and then a guy, which I figured must be a college devil bustin' into a new fraternity, comes gallopin' across the floor, slams a suitcase down on my foot and throws his arms around the wife's neck. He had on a cap which could of been used as a checker board when you got tired of wearin' it, a suit of clothes that must of been made by a maniac tailor and the yellowest tan shoes I ever seen in my life. If he had been three inches taller and an ounce thinner, you could of put a tent around him and got a dime admission. On his upper lip, which was of a retirin' disposition, he had a mustache that was an outright steal from Chaplin.

I watched him and my wife embrace as long as I could stand it and then I tapped her on the shoulder.

"I suppose this is Alex, eh?" I says—while he looks at me for the first time.

"You got Sherlock Holmes lookin' stupid!" admits the wife. "Alex, meet my lord and master."

"Howdy, cousin!" hollers Alex. "I knowed you the minute I seen you from them, now, big ears you got. Y'know they went to work and printed your picture in the Sunday papers last month on a charge of havin' won the, now, pennant for—Well, that's neither here nor there. I come here to make good! A feller with brains can always do that in these big rube towns like New York. Of course a baseball player don't need no brains—you know that yourself and—"

"C'mon, Alex," butts in the wife quickly, seein' I was gettin' ready to grab Alex by the neck. "We'll go right up to the flat and have something to eat. I'll bet you haven't had a bite since you left home— you ought to be starved by this time!"

"I'd rather see him shot, myself!" I growls, taggin' along after them, carryin' this bird's suitcase. If they was clothes in there, Alex must of dressed in armor up in Vermont. The thing was as heavy as two dollars' worth of corn beef and cabbage. However, I figured I'd get back at Alex the minute he asked me for a job. I was all set for this bird, believe me!

"So this is New York, hey?" he pipes through his nose the minute we get outside the station. He stops dead in the street, gazin' up at the big buildin's and then down at the crowds like a guy in a trance. All he needed was a streamer of hay in his mouth and the first seven guys that passed would of offered to sell him the Bronx. He gasps a couple of times and wipes his eyes.

"Well, Alex," I says, tryin' hard not to laugh in his face, "what d'ye think of New York? Considerable burg, eh?"

He shakes his head kinda sad and sighs.

"I'll speak plain to you, cousin," he says. "Of all the rube burgs I ever seen, this here's the limit!"

I liked to fell down one of them Subway holes!

"Rube town?" I yells. "Where d'ye get that stuff? Are you seekin' to kid me?"

He grabs me by the shoulders and swings me around.

8

"Just you look at that crowd of folks on the corner there!" he tells me. He points over to where half New York is bein' held up in a traffic jam—wagons, autos, surface cars and guys usin' rubber heels as a means of locomotion, all waitin' for the cop to say, "Go!"

"Just look at 'em!" repeats Alex, sneering at me. "From the reports that have reached me, this here's the town where all the brains in the world is gathered. There's a couple hundred of them brains on the corner there now, I reckon, and they can't go nowheres till that constabule gives the word! Huh!" he snorts, turnin' away. "All just a lot of rubes, that's all!"

We get in a taxi and all the way up Alex kept lookin' out the window, shakin' his head and mutterin' somethin' about Manhattan bein' a well-advertised bunk and all the inhabitants thereof bein' hicks. I don't know whether he was after my goat or not, but in a few minutes he had it.

"Listen, gentle stranger," I says, when nature could stand no more, "I realize that New York is nothin' but a flag station and that we're all Reubens and chew hay, but we have, amongst other things, six million merry villagers, the biggest buildings in the world, the subway, gunmen, cabarets, Broadway, and—well, a lot of things that you gotta admit ain't hit dear old Vermont as yet!"

"And I most sincerely hope and trust they never will!" pipes Alex. "We don't need 'em! We got good, clean mountain air, plenty of honest green grass and—and—*neighbors*! There's just a few things you ain't got in New York. Cousin Alice tells me she was here two years before she knowed the folks in the next flat. That shows you people is suspicious. You know you're rubes and you're afraid to welcome the stranger for fear he'll sell you one of them, now, gold bricks. I also hear you pay five and six dollars for a seat at an entertainment. You so-called wise New Yorkers pays that much for tickets and then go in and laugh your fool heads off at a scene showin' a, now, farmer bein' stung! Ha, ha, ha! You—"

We was up at the flat then, and I let him rave on, tryin' not to get peeved, so's we'd have some peace and quiet in the family. I knew if he kept on pannin' my town, I'd get sore and bite him or somethin'—and then the wife wouldn't gimme no smile for a month. Alex was a new one on me so far, but I figured that in a couple of days he'd be tellin' the world that New York was the greatest place on earth and people that lived anywheres else must be nutty—the way they all do.

After supper the wife calls up a girl friend of hers so's we can make up a little theatre party. Me and Alex goes into the parlor for a smoke, and I asked him how he come to be in our mongst if he already knowed what a hick town New York was.

"I come here to make good," he tells me, "because, in my opinion, this is the easiest place in the world to do that thing. This town is no different than Ann Harbor or New Haven, except that it's bigger— that's all! The trouble with most fellows that come here from a small town is, they let New York get under their skin and it takes their nerve before they get started. Advertisin' is what has made this town what it is to-day and nothin' else. It's easier to make good here than it is in a burg, because in your own town everybody knows you and now fourflushin' will get you nothin'. There's so many people here that a feller can keep *some* of 'em guessin' all the time. All anybody needs to get ahead here is confidence—"

"Well," I butts in, "if all a guy needs is confidence, you ought to be a knockout! What are you figurin' on doin' first?"

"I'll look around to-morrow," he says. "I wanna start off with the hardest proposition in the town right away. Out in my town five of us fellers formed a little club. Each of us has swore to come to New York one after the other and make good in six months to a year, just to show you folks how easy it is. For one thing, we all got our own private little plans for winnin' out here and every one of us is goin' to go at the proposition from a brand new angle. I was elected to be the first one, and that's why I'm here."

"Alex," I says, "you're an ambitious feller, and I gotta hand it to you. I don't doubt you'll go a long ways at that, if you don't get pinched for speedin'. But this stuff you're pullin' about dear old Manhattan gets under my collar! I hate to hear you pan the capital of the world in that rough way of yours, and when you claim it's a simple matter to make good here, you have gone and pulled a bone. If it's as soft as you say, I must of lost the combination or somethin', because it took me thirty years to get over right here, and, at that, I ain't causin' Rockefeller or George M. Cohan no worry! So just to show you that your dope is all wrong and that you're due to hit the bumps if you play it out, I'll lay you eight to five you muff the very first thing you try here—what d'ye say?"

He looks at me for a minute and shakes his head.

"I don't want to deprive my Cousin Alice of no luxuries," he tells me, "or I'd snap you right up on that."

"I see they're still makin' 'em yellah up in Vermont!" I sneers.

"D'ye mean to insinuate that I'm a quitter?" he asks me, gettin' red.

"You ought to be a fortune teller!" I says.

"By gravy, I'll take you up!" he hollers. "I got five hundred dollars in my left shoe and I might as well add to it now as later. I'll bet you the five hundred to your eight hundred that the first thing I tackle here, I make good!"

"You hate yourself, don't you?" I says.

"Who's yellah now?" he comes back.

"The canary," I tells him. "You're on!"

Just then the door-bell rings, and they was sounds of kissin' by women principals in the hall. In walks the wife with what looks to me like a opium-eater's dream and a Fifth Avenue evenin' gown model combined. Alex takes one flash and turns red, white and blue.

"This is my friend Eve Rossiter," says the wife. "My husband, Eve, and my cousin, Alex Hanley."

"Charmed!" breathes Eve, pullin' a smile that lit up the room.

"Me and you both!" I says.

But Alex clears his throat, grits his teeth and flushes up. They was a glitter in his eye and he begins to talk fast and hard.

"Howdy, Miss Rossiter!" he says, shakin' hands like he was bein' give a knockdown to the new bartender. "I'm astounded to meet you! I just come to New York to-day, but if I'd of knowed you was here, I'd of been here long ago. However, I'm here now and better late than forever, as the feller says. I just bet my cousin here that the first thing I tried my hand at in New York I'd make good. I'm goin' out to-morrow and show him how easy it is for a feller to get to the top in this here prize rube burg, provided he has now gumption and his methods is new. I'll see you to-morrow night and let you know how I made out; I know you won't have no peace till you hear about it!" He digs into his pockets feverishly and grabs out a handful of letters. "Here's what they thought of me up in Vermont!" he goes on, never takin' his eyes off the girl's face. The wife is starin' at him with her mouth and eyes as open as a crap tourney, like she figured he'd gone nutty—and me and Little Eva is runnin' neck and neck at tryin' to keep from laughin'. "They say a man that can make good in New York can make good anywhere," he goes on, throwin' the clutch into high again. "I say a man that can make good anywhere can make good in New York! What's the difference between New York and Goose Creek, Iowa?—New York's got more people in it, that's all! It's harder—"

"Alex, Alex!" butts in the wife, finally regainin' control of her voice. "What is the matter with you? You—"

"Hush!" says Alex, turnin' back to Eve again. "It's harder to make good in a little town than it is in a big one, because —"

"Alex, look here!" cuts in the wife, gettin' sore. "Miss Rossiter ain't interested in that patter of yours — we're goin' to the theatre. Now both you men run along and dress, we'll miss half the show as it is!"

"I'll be right back!" chirps Alex to Eve. "Them eyes of yours is simply now dumfoundin'!"

I took Alex in my boudoir and while I'm gettin' in the banquet uneyform, he takes a thing that was a cross between a tuxedo and a dress suit out of his bag and dolls up. When set for the street, Alex was no Greek god, but he was fairly easy to look at, if you closed one eye. He wanted to know what kind of an entertainment they had at the opry house this week, and I told him I'd show him somethin' that had them huskin' bees, he was used to up in Vermont, beat eighty ways from the jack.

Well, we go to the biggest musical show on Broadway, and instead of faintin' dead away from joy, Alex claims it was rotten and spent the night explainin' to Eve how he was gonna take New York the next mornin'. After the show we went to a cabaret and still no rise out of Alex. He was off the gay whirl, he says, and his idea of a holiday was to sit beside his own fireside, readin' yesterday's mail, while his wife made the room resound with melody by hummin' "Silver Threads Among The Gold," the while knittin' a doily for the front-room table.

At this, Eve, which has been gazin' at Alex all night like he was Coney Island and she was gettin' her first peep, asks if he was married.

"Don't crowd me!" he tells her, tappin' her arm playfully. "I ain't gonna get married till I make good. By to-morrow night, though, I reckon I'll be in a position to talk it over with you!"

"Ooooh!!" gasps Eve, turnin' a becomin' shade of red. Can you tell me why them big league dames fall for these guys like Alex? If you can do that, I got an easy one for you—I wanna know who started the world. From one flash at Eve, bein' a married man, I could tell where she'd be the next night when Alex called—and it wouldn't be—out! The next minute Eve laughed and tells Alex if he's got as much ability as he has nerve, he ought to have New York on its ear in twenty-four hours. The wife asks him will he kindly lay off pesterin' her girl friend to death and quit boostin' himself for a minute, because we was out for pleasure and he had played the one record all night.

"Go on, Mister Hanley," butts in Eve, "I love to hear you talk. You're so different from any one else I've met, and I really believe you *will* do something big here, because you're—well—new!"

"You have remarked somethin'!" agrees Alex. "I'm gonna show 'em somethin' they never seen before and make 'em like it!"

Well, he takes Eve home that night for a starter, and the next mornin' he's up bright and early at seven, ready to startle Manhattan. He said he wanted me to go out with him and watch him win my eight hundred bucks and also to notice the way he worked. He picks up the mornin' paper, runs through the "Help Wanted" columns for a minute and finally clears his throat.

"Aha!" he says. "Listen to this—'Wanted. High class automobile salesman for the Gaflooey light delivery wagon. We have no time for experiments and successful applicant must make good at once. We don't want an order taker, but an order *maker*—a real, live, simon-pure hustler who will start delivering the goods the morning he goes on the payroll. This job pays ten thousand a year, if you show us you're worth it. Apply personally all day and bring references. This is imperative. We want to see your past record of sales elsewhere. Ask for Mr. Grattan, 1346 Broadway. If you haven't the experience, don't come!'"

"Well?" I says.

He puts down the paper and reaches for his hat.

"They'll probably be a lot after that there job, hey?" he asks me.

"About four thousand, I'd say offhand!" I grins.

"Fine!" he says, rubbin' his hands and smilin', "I love competition because it puts a feller on his mettle. Now look here, if I go down there and secure that job this mornin', do I get your eight hundred dollars?"

"What?" I hollers. "What d'ye mean, do you get my eight hundred?"

"Listen!" he says. "The bet was that I make good at the first thing I tackle, wasn't it—all right! Now this here job looks good to me. Ten thousand a year is nice money to start. If you're fair minded, you'll admit that in goin' after this job I'm up against a pretty stiff proposition. In the first place I don't know no more about automobiles than you do about raisin' hogs. I never sold one in my life. I don't know a soul in New York outside of you, Cousin Alice and that girl I took home last night, so I can't furnish no references on my ability as a salesman. The advertisement says you have to have 'em. As you say, they'll be thousands after that job. Fellers with swell fronts, high soundin' records in back of 'em and gilt-edged references. Now under all that handicap, if I walk in there and get the job, won't you admit I made good?"

"If you go down and ask for that job and they turn you down, you'll pay me, eh?" I asks him.

"At once!" he says, firmly.

"C'mon, Alex!" I tells him, puttin' on my hat. "I hate to cop a sucker bet like this, but maybe losin' it will reduce the size of your head a trifle and do you good!"

Once out in the street, he stretches his arms, pulls his hat down hard over his dome and stamps his feet.

"Watch me close!" he says. "Watch me close and you'll get some valuable tips on how to put yourself over. I told you I was gonna be new—just observe how I go after this job. The average New Yorker who wanted it would go right down to the office, present his, now, credentials and ask for it, wouldn't he?"

I nodded.

"The early worm catches the fish, y'know!" I says; "and in New York here—the town that made pep and hustle famous—a man would be down there at six a.m. waitin' for the place to open. Why, there's prob'ly a hundred or more there right now!"

"I hope there's a million!" he comes back. "It'll be more satisfaction when they hire me over all them others. Now I ain't goin' near that there office as yet. My system gets away from the old stuff—just keep your eye on Cousin Alex from now on!"

He buys a newspaper, finds the automobile section and, finally, a big display advertisement of the Gaflooey Auto Company. He takes out a letter from his pocket and on the back of it he marks the price, style, and a lot of other dope about Gaflooey light delivery wagons and then throws the paper away.

"Now," he grins, "I'm all ready, except to give them folks my full name for the payroll!"

At that minute, somebody slaps me on the back and I swing around to see Buck Rice chucklin' at me. Buck used to be one of the best second basemen that ever picked up a bat, till his legs went back on him and he got into the automobile game. I remember thinkin' how funny it was that he come along right then when me and Alex was talkin' about autos.

"Well, how are they breakin', Buck?" I says, shakin' hands and introducin' Alex.

"I think I have fanned with the bases loaded again," he laughs. "I put in five hours to-day tryin' to get the Mastadon Department Store to put in a line of six-cylinder Katzes on their delivery system. I got a private tip that they're changin' from the Mutz-36 and the first order will be about eighty cars. Of course that's a sweet piece of money for somebody and everybody in New York will be there to-day tryin' to grab that order off. You might as well try to sell radiators in Hades though, because Munson, the bird that does the purchasin', is stuck on the Clarendon and he wouldn't buy anything else if they was givin' 'em away!"

"Well, that's tough, Buck!" I sympathizes.

"Sure is!" he says, givin' me and Alex a quarter perfecto and grinnin' some more to show how disappointed he feels. "But I should worry! If I lose that one, I'll get another, so what's the difference?" He turns to Alex, "Y'know in New York here," he confides, "we don't have no time to hold no coroner's inquests over failures. We forget about 'em and go after somethin' else—always on the job, get me? You'll learn after you're here a while—that's what makes the town what it is. If I stopped to moan over every order I didn't put across, I'd be nowhere to-day. Nope, you can't do that in New York!"

"Another of them there New Yorkers, hey?" sneers Alex to me, after Buck has blowed. "Don't you see how that feller proves my argyment about how simple it is to make good here? From the way he's dressed—them, now, diamonds and so forth—he's probably a big feller in his line. Makin' plenty of money and looked on as a success by the ig'rant. Yet he lets a big order get away from him when it was practically a cinch to land it!"

"Say, listen!" I yelps—this bird was gettin' on my nerves. "If four-flushin' was water, you'd be the Pacific Ocean! You gimme a pain with that line of patter you got, and as far as salesmanship is concerned, I'll bet you couldn't sell a porterhouse steak to a guy dyin' of hunger. I'd like to see *you* land an order like Buck spoke of, you—"

17

"That's just what you're gonna do!" he butts in. "You're gonna see *me* land that very order he told us about—what d'ye think of that, hey?"

I stopped dead and gazed upon him.

"You're gonna which?" I asks him.

"I'm gonna land that order from that department store!" he repeats, grabbin' my arm. "C'mon—show me how to get there!"

I fell up against a lamp post and laughed till a passin' dame remarked to her friend that it was an outrage the way some guys drank. Then I led Alex to the subway.

"Listen," I says. "What about this job you was gonna get? Of course you know if you quit, I win the bet."

"Quit?" he says. "Where have I heard the word before? Who said anything about quittin'? I'm gonna get that order and I'm gonna get that job!"

"Fair enough!" I tells him, "but you're goin' at the thing backwards. How are you gonna take an order for autos when you ain't got no autos to sell? I suppose you figure on grabbin' the ten thousand dollar job first and then makin' good with a loud crash by landin' the big order, eh?"

He shakes his head and sighs pityin'ly.

"Would there be anything new and original about that?" he asks.

"No!" I says, "there wouldn't! But I don't see how you're gonna win out any other way."

"Of course you don't!" he sneers. "You're a New Yorker, ain't you? I'm supposed to be the rube, simply because I wasn't born on Sixth Avenue. Now I already told you my methods was new, didn't I?

Anybody would work the thing the way you lay it out—and probably land neither the job nor the order. What a chance would I have goin' up there and askin' for that job first? Where would I come out against all them sellin' experts with letters and so forth to prove it? Why, they'd laugh me outa the office! *B-u-t!—if I go to them with an order for fifty or sixty of their cars as actual proof that I can sell not only autos, but their autos,* what will they say, then? D'ye see the point now? They ask me for a reference and I reach in my pocket and give them the order, *which I've got before applyin' for the job,* to prove to myself and them that I can sell automobiles!"

Oh, boy!

"Alex," I says, when I got my breath, "I gotta hand it to you! When it comes to inventin' things, you got Edison lookin' like a backward pupil. Go to it, old kid! If you put this over the way you have just told it to me, you'll own Broadway in a week!"

"I'm figurin' on ten days!" he says.

We arrive at the Mastadon Department Store and shoot up in the elevator to the office of G. C. Munson, the general manager. Alex has been readin' the notes he made on Gaflooey delivery wagons like the same was a French novel, and, by the time we got there, he could repeat their advertisement by heart. He starts to breeze right into the office and some dame appears on the scene and nails him.

"One moment, please!" she says, very cold—givin' Alex a look that took in everything from his hick clothes to his rube haircut. "This happens to be a private office. Whom did you desire to see?"

"If I thought they was anybody prettier than you here, I'd ask to have them brought out," says Alex, in that simple rube way of his which give no offense, "but of course I know that's impossible. Still, as long as I'm here, I'd like to see Mister Munson."

The dame melts and releases a smile.

19

"What did you wish to see him about?" she asks.

"About ten minutes," pipes Alex. "D'ye know there's somethin' about them navy blue eyes of yours that makes me think of my mother—isn't that funny?"

The dame surrenders and shows Alex all her nice front teeth.

"I'll see if Mister Munson is in," she says, handin' him a card, "but you'll have to fill this out."

Alex looks at the card which had this on it,

Mr ....

Desires to see ....

Regarding ....

He laughs suddenly, takes out his fountain pen and fills the thing out. Lookin' over his shoulder I seen him write this,

Mr......... *Alex Hanley*

Desires to see ...... *Mr. Munson.*

Regarding .... *The price of petrified noodles in Siberia.*

"There," he says, handin' it to the girl without a smile, "give that to Mister Munson."

She takes it in without lookin' at it.

"Well, you crabbed any chance you might of had, right off the bat!" I says to Alex. "He'll get so sore when he reads that, he won't even let you in."

"Let him get sore!" chirps Alex. "He'll not only get sore, he'll get curious and then again I'm figurin' on him bein' human, besides bein' general manager and havin' a sense of humor! He's probably been pestered with auto salesmen all day—if I wrote my real business on that card he'd send word he was out. As it is, he'll read it and he won't be able to resist the, now, temptation to get one look at a feller which would want to know from a man in his position the price of petrified noodles in Siberia. No matter what happens afterwards, he'll want one look—wouldn't you?"

Before I can answer, the dame comes out laughin'.

"Step in," she says. "Mister Munson will see you."

"Now!" hisses Alex, as we ease in on the velvet carpet. "Watch how *I* go about sellin' autos. Y'see I got a nibble already because I was new! I—Howdy, Mister Munson!"

We was in the private office.

Munson was a little, keen-faced guy—bald, nervous and fat. He looks up over his glasses with Alex's card in his hand—and Alex looks back. In one second they had each found out all they wanted to know about the other.

"What's the meaning of this nonsense?" barks Munson.

Alex walks over to the desk, wets his lips and gets goin'.

"Mister Munson," he says, "if you called on a man at his office, would you care to write your business on a card for the office boy to read? No—you would not! A big man like you would probably tear the card up, leave the office in a, now, rage and never return! You'd be insulted, your, now, dignity would be hurt, eh? You might be from out of town and comin' here to leave a big order and that little thing—prob'ly invented by one of your New York efficiency stars— would make you so mad you'd go away and order where they wasn't so efficient, but a little more courteous! Look at that card—

the, now, wordin' of it. Look how cold and hard it is! No warmth, no 'glad-to-see-you-stranger what-can-my-house-do-for-you?' about it. It's like a slap in the face! Maybe it does keep the panhandlers away, but did you ever figure how many orders it must have cost you, hey?"

Munson has listened to every word, first with a heavy frown and then with a kind of thoughtful look on his face. He taps the desk with a lead pencil, reads the card a couple of times and then slams his fist on the desk.

"By Peter, young man!" he snaps out suddenly, "you may be right! The wording of that office blank *is* rather insulting, now that I dissect it—been too busy before to notice it. Yes, sir, I *would* resent having my business blatted out before a whole staff of subordinates! There must be some way, of course, to keep out the hordes of jobless and what not who would get in if it wasn't for that blank and now, by the eternal, we'll find one less liable to turn away gold with the—er—grist! I thank you for the suggestion. And now, what did you want to see me about?"

"Automobiles," says Alex, "and—"

Munson freezes right up and slaps his hands together.

"That's enough!" he snarls. "Perhaps that office blank of ours is not so bad after all! If you had filled it out properly, you wouldn't be here. I've heard enough about autos to-day to last me for the rest of my life. Yesterday, I mentioned casually, and I thought in confidence, that we were considering a change in our delivery system. Beginning at eight this morning, there has been a constant stream of automobile salesmen in this office! The only persons who have not tried to sell me automobiles are George Washington, Jack Dempsey and Billy Sunday! I'm quite sure every one else has been here. The air has been filled with magnetos, self-starters, sliding gear transmissions, aluminum crank cases and all that other damnable technical stuff that goes with automobiles! You need not open your mouth—I know exactly what your sales talk is, they're all alike, more or less. Your car is far and away the best on the market, of course, and—"

"Excuse me, Mister Munson!" butts in Alex. "You get me all wrong. Our car—the Gaflooey—is *not* the best on the market. There are others just as good and some of the higher priced ones are, naturally, better. You can't expect the best on the market for the price we sell at—750. A man of your intelligence knows that and when a salesman tells you his five hundred dollar car is better than a standard make at five thousand, he's insulting your intelligence. We make a good, honest car—that's all. I ain't gonna take up your time tellin' you about the—eh—ah—the—eh, magneto and so forth. Unless you're a mechanic, you wouldn't understand about 'em anyways. All the parts that go with any car are on ours, or it wouldn't work—that's understood. However, as I said before, I ain't gonna take up your time. I know how you New Yorkers do business, and you've probably made your mind up already. You big men are all zip!—like that. Mind made up and nothin' can change you. Even if you do miss somethin' good now and then, you don't mind because you have the satisfaction of bein' known as a quick thinker. We just got in a new consignment of cars to-day and if you're interested our place is at 1346 Broadway. Well, good-day, sir!" he winds up, reachin' for his hat.

"Wait!" says Munson, takin' off his glasses and wipin' 'em. "You're a new one on me, son! So you admit you haven't got the greatest auto that was ever made, eh?" he chuckles. "By Peter! That sounds strange after all the talk I been listening to to-day. If your car is as honest as you seem to be, it's all right!" He sits lookin' off in the air, tappin' the desk with the pencil again.

Alex nudges me and we start for the door. Halfway he stops and looks at a photo that's framed over the desk. It's a picture of a barn, some chickens and a couple of cows.

"Right fine landscape, that!" chirps Alex to Munson. "Makes a feller like me homesick to look at it. Them are sure fine Jerseys, too—and say, see them pullets, would you!"

"That's my little farm down on Long Island," says Munson, throwin' out his chest. "I suppose that makes you laugh, eh? Big, grown New Yorker having a farm, eh?"

"Mister," says Alex, sadly, "it don't make *me* laugh! I was raised on a farm in Vermont and—"

"That so?" cuts in Munson, lookin' interested. "Country boy, eh?"

"Yep," goes on Alex. "Now, speakin' of them pullets there—if you'd try 'em on a straight diet of bran and potatoes—pound of each—they'll fatten up quicker."

"Yes?" pipes Munson, brightenin' up some more. "Well, well! And—hmph! Thanks, Mister Hanley, I'll make a note of that. Now—eh—sit down a minute! I don't want to take your time, but—eh, what did you find best back home for saving the young chicks? What foods—"

"I'll just leave you a few little rules," says Alex, his eyes glitterin', as he rams his elbow a mile in my ribs. "I got to call on another department store this afternoon, where I'm almost certain to take an order and—"

"Young man!" Munson shuts him off, "I'm frank enough to say that you've made a very favorable impression on me. You're honest about your car, and you didn't try to overawe me by hurling a lot of unintelligible technical terms into my ear. You don't claim it's the bargain of the age. Now we have recently inaugurated right here in this store a policy of absolute honesty with regard to our merchandise. No misrepresentations are permitted. We sell our goods for what they are—we don't allow a clerk to tell a customer that he's getting a five-dollar shirt for two dollars. I can't get the car I want to put in here—they want too much money and their salesman spent most of his time here speaking in terms that none but a master mechanic on their own auto would understand. I'm a pretty good judge of character and you look good to me. Give me a price on fifty of your cars for immediate delivery and—well, let's hear your figures!"

Alex drops his hat on the floor, but when he picked it up, he was as cool as a dollar's worth of ice.

"Just a minute," he says, sittin' down and reachin' for a desk telephone. He gets the Gaflooey Company on the wire.

"Hello!" he says. "Say—I want a lump price on fifty delivery wagons—what?—never mind who this is, if the price is right I'll come up." He winks at Munson like he's lettin' him in on somethin'—and, by gravy, Munson winks back! "Yes—fifty," says Alex on the wire. "Thirty-five thousand dollars?—thank you!" He hangs up the phone and turns to Munson. "They'll give you twenty-five hundred off, accordin' to that figure," he says.

Munson grabs up a pad and writes somethin' on it.

"There!" he says, givin' it to Alex. "Tell 'em to get as many cars over here to-morrow as they can. Get your bill and I'll O.K. it. Now—" he pulls his chair over closer, "About those chicks and—oh, yes, I want your opinion on some figures I have here on my truck—"

An hour later, me and Alex walks into the salesroom of the Gaflooey Automobile Company. I was in a trance, and if he had of promised to lift the Singer Buildin' with one hand I would of laid the world eight to five he could do it! The whole place is in confusion—salesmen chasin' around, telephonin' and actin' like they just heard they was a bomb in the basement. Alex asks for the manager, and some guy chances over and asks what he wants.

"I have come for that ten thousand a year job you advertised this mornin'," says Alex.

"Job?" howls the manager, glarin' at him. "You poor boob, can't you see how busy we are here now? We just got a tip on a real order—fifty cars, and we can't trace the thing!" He rubs his hands together. "Fifty cars! That's how the Gaflooey sells—fifty at a time!" He sneers at Alex. "Your approach is terrible!" he says. "You'll never land a job in this town like that, my boy. Go somewhere first and learn how to interest a busy man with the first thing you say and—"

"Listen!" butts in Alex. "Gimme that job, will you, or I'll have to go somewhere else."

The manager laughs, as a couple of salesmen come along and join him. They all sneer at Alex and the manager nudges his minions and winks.

"So you think you're a ten thousand dollar auto salesman, eh?" he says. "Ah—who can you refer to?" He makes a bluff at takin' down notes.

"Mister Munson, of the Mastadon Department Store," says Alex.

"Ha, ha, ha!" roars the manager. "Department store, eh—that's rich! You quit the shirtwaist department to sell autos, eh? Ha, ha, ha! What does a department store manager know of your ability to sell autos?" he snarls.

"Well,—I just sold him fifty of *yours!*" remarks Alex. "So I thought—"

"What?" shrieks the manager, grabbin' his arm.

Alex hands over the order Munson give him.

"Now before I go to work here," he says, "it might be a good idea to let me look over one of your cars, because, to tell you the truth, I ain't never seen one of 'em in my life!"

Well, they had Munson on the phone in a minute and in another one the manager hangs up the receiver and comes back.

"Do I get the job?" asks Alex.

"Do you get the job!" yells friend manager, slappin' him on the back. "No, you don't get it—only if you leave here without signing your name to a five-year contract and accepting a check for fifteen hundred dollars' commission and as much more as you want to draw on your expense account, I'll—I'll—murder you! But first, you lunch with me at the Fitz-Barlton and we'll map out a campaign—"

"Gimme that eight hundred!" says Alex to me.

I passed it over still semi-conscious.

Alex stretches his arms, puts the money away and grins.

"Get me that Eve girl on the phone, will you?" he tells me. "I—I had a little bet with her, too!" He lights the cigar Buck Rice had give him in the mornin', blows out some smoke and looks over at Broadway, jammed with the matinée crowd. "Some burg!" he says, shakin' his head and grinnin' at me!

CHAPTER II

THE SELF-COMMENCER

There's nothin' the world loves so much as a good tryer. I don't mean the birds that havin' everything in their favor, includin' a ten-mile start, finishes first in the Big Race—I'm talkin' about the guys that never get better than second or third, but generally land in the money. The old Consistent Charlies that, no matter how many times they're beaten, figures the time to quit is when you're dead and buried!

Did you ever stop to think that the tryers which never get nowhere is responsible for the other guys' success? They're the babies that make a race or a fight out of it, and if it wasn't for them dubs there'd be no successes at all. In order to have winners, we got to have *losers*, don't we? And don't forget that yesterday's losers are to-morrow's winners and vice-president or vice versa, whatever it is.

A fighter knows that these birds which come up smilin' no matter how many times he drops 'em for the count is as dangerous as dynamite, until he knocks 'em cold. No matter how bad this loser may be battered up, he's always got a chance while he's tryin'. I've seen guys that was winnin' by two miles curl up and quit before a dub they had beaten till the crowd was yellin' for mercy, simply because this poor bunged-up simp kept comin' in all the time— battered, bloody, drunk with wallops—*but tryin' up to the last bell*!

Now these guys may never get nowhere, but they're the birds that's put most of the guys that *do* where they are. Why? Think it over! You gotta be *good* to beat them birds, don't you? They make competition keen, they keep the other guys on their toes, they're the gasoline that keeps the old world goin' forward on high and the birds that get over are only the chauffeurs. You gotta have both to run the car and the universe wouldn't move forward six inches if we didn't have one failure for every success.

So if you've failed to set the world on fire up to date, don't walk out on the dock to see what kind of a jump it is. If you can't be a winner, you can be a good loser and it's a toss-up which is the bigger thing! A guy who can beat the yellah streak we all pack somewheres, every time he fails to register a win, and will keep rememberin' that tomorrow has got yesterday beat eighty-seven ways, is no loser! On paper he mightn't be a winner, but he *is*. He's a bigger winner than the bird that gets over, because he's whipped the quit in him without no kind applause to cheer him on. I've seen losers that attracted more attention in runnin' *last* than any six winners in the same precinct.

Them kind of birds can't help tryin'. They couldn't quit if they wanted to, which they don't! They got somethin' in 'em that keeps shovin' 'em along whether they're regrettin' the breaks or not. They're always full of the old ambish no matter what the score is in the ninth. They're what you might call self-starters in the automobile of life—they don't need a *win* now and then to crank 'em up, they keep goin' forward hittin' on all cylinders from the nursery to the embalmer!

Alex was one of them guys.

The Big Town fell for his stuff because it was *new*, the same as it will fall for *yours* to-morrow if you get somethin' it never seen and the nerve to try it out!

About a month after Alex was workin' as head salesman for the Gaflooey Auto Company at a pittance of ten thousand a year, he come up to the flat for dinner one night. I seen right away that somethin' was wrong, because he only eat about half of the roast duck and brung along his own cigars. After nature could stand no more, and we had dragged ourselves away from the table to let the servant girl make good, we adjourn to the parlor and the wife gets ready to punish the neighbors with the victrola.

"Well," says Alex, sittin' down in the only rocker, of course, "it looks like they have finally gimme somethin' that even *I* can't do!"

"Can that be possible?" I says, pickin' up the sportin' final.

"Wait till you hear this one!" remarks the wife, crankin' up the victrola. "John McCormack singin' 'If Beauty Was Water, You'd Be Niagara Falls!' It's a knockout!"

"Say!" snorts Alex, gettin' peeved. "Can't a man find no attention here?"

"Look in the telephone book under the A's," I says.

"Never mind, dearie!" the wife tells him. "I'll listen. What's on your mind?" She goes over and sits on the arm of his chair, knowin' full well it gets my goat.

"I see you're the only one in this family that's got any sense!" pipes Alex, pattin' her hand.

"Yen," I says, "I ain't got enough sense to turn on a radiator. All I'm good for is to get the dollars, which of course is nothin' at all in keepin' up the home!"

"Well, you'll never have Rockefeller and that crowd gnashin' their teeth with all the dollars you'll get!" says Alex, "and that ain't no lie!"

"Now, boys," butts in the wife, "let's all be friends even if we do belong to the same family. What is it, Alex? Speak up like a man."

"Well," he says, "the Gaflooey people has started to make tourin' cars and roadsters! What d'ye think of that?"

"I'm simply dumfounded!" I says. "Has Congress heard about this?"

"There you go again!" snorts Alex. "Always tryin' to ridicule everything I do. It's simply a case of sour grapes with you—jealousy, that's all!"

"Sour grapes ain't jealousy," I says. "Sour grapes is brandy. Go on with your story, Alex."

"Don't mind him," whispers the wife in his ear. "He'd laugh in church!"

"Why not?" I says. "I ain't done no gigglin' since you and me first went there together."

"Will you let go?" she says. "Go on, Alex."

"Well," he says, "they called me into the president's office to-day, and the former begins by tellin' me I'm the best salesman they ever had."

"He don't care what he says, does he?" I butts in. "I suppose you admitted the charge, eh?"

"After that," goes on Alex, snubbin' me, "he tells me they have decided to get into the pleasure car game, instead of just makin' trucks and the like. Their first offerin' is gonna be one of them chummy, clover-leaf roadsters which will hold five people comfortably."

"If they're well acquainted!" I says.

"Will you leave the boy alone?" asks the wife. "I never saw anybody like you in my life!"

"Don't I know it?" I says. "Otherwise, how would we ever of got married?"

"Now," goes on Alex, "they want me to go up and see Runyon Q. Sampson, the well-to-do millionaire, and get him to buy the first car. You can imagine what a terrible good advertisement that will be for us if he should buy it, can't you?"

"It'll be O.K. till he tries to ride in it," I says, "and then the chances are you'll have to leave town and the Gaflooey people will be facin' a suit!"

"There ain't another car on the market that can hold a match to the Gaflooey!" hollers Alex, his goat prancin' madly about.

"What's it made out of—celluloid?" I says.

"You may think you're funny!" he tells me, "but that's nothin' more or less than ig'rance. Here I am wastin' valuable time tryin' to explain somethin' to Cousin Alice and you keep interruptin' till a man don't know where he's at! Let's see now, where was I?" he asks the wife.

"The beautiful and good-lookin' princess had just promised to wed you," I says, "but the crusty old king couldn't see into it!"

The wife throws a pillow at me and it busted a vase that cost me three hundred green certificates. After a short brawl over the remains, I laid off Alex and he went ahead.

"As I said before," he goes on, "the president of the Gaflooey Company has selected me to go up and sell old Sampson this here chummy roadster. If I land the order, which naturally enough I will, it means I get made manager of the New York salesrooms. Then me and Eve Rossiter will prob'ly get married and—"

"What?" squeals the wife. "Are you and Eve engaged? And she never said a word to me!"

"How could she?" I says. "When he prob'ly had her doped?"

"No, we ain't engaged," says Alex. "I ain't even asked the girl will she be mine yet."

"Then how do you know she'll marry you?" asks the wife.

"Well," says Alex, "I figure if you married this here pest, I ought to be able to marry anybody! But what I'm up against is this—I got to take one of them roadsters up there to-day and demonstrate it to Sampson. They have gone to work and made an appointment for me, and what I don't know about automobiles would fill seven large libraries. Here I'm supposed to show Mister Sampson the points on our car which is better than any other and I can't tell the windshield from the magneto. Now d'ye blame me for bein' worried?"

"I thought you was the world's greatest salesman," I sneers. "You don't mean to say this job has got you yellin' for the police already, do you? What are you gonna do, quit?"

"Speak English!" he comes back. "That word quit don't belong in our language. Who said anything about quittin'? Even though I don't know a thing about automobiles, I'm gonna sell Runyon Q. Sampson a Gaflooey chummy roadster. A feller don't need knowledge to be a success half as much as he needs confidence and I got more confidence than a feller shootin' at a barn with a double-barrelled shot gun. Anyhow, I'll betcha a rich millionaire like Sampson don't know any too much about automobiles himself, bein' too busy with makin' money and the like, eh?"

"I suppose you're gonna make him think that you know more about them gas buckboards than the guy which wrote 'em, eh?" I says.

"You'll never get nowhere!" he answers, lookin' at me like how can a guy live and be so thick behind the ears. "You'll never be nothin' but an average citizen, because you never get a new idea! No, I ain't gonna make Sampson think *I* know more about automobiles than anybody in the world—that's what has queered many a sale. I'm gonna make him think *he* does, and that him buyin' our roadster proves it!"

"I'll bet you could make Rockefeller think they wasn't a nickel in oil!" says the wife admirin'ly.

Alex gets up and reaches for his hat.

"If they was enough money in it for me, I'd try it," he says, "and that ain't no lie!"

I didn't see Alex till the next mornin' and then he blows in the flat.

"Hello!" he says. "Here you are as usual, loafin' away the hull mornin'. It's almost eight o'clock, d'ye know that?"

"Sure!" I says. "You can't get me on that one. The answer is seven fifty-five!"

"What d'ye mean, seven fifty-five?" he asks.

"Ain't seven fifty-five almost eight o'clock," I says, "and didn't you ask me if I knew it?"

"Ain't he clever?" says the wife, pattin' me on the back.

Alex looks at me in open disgust.

"If that's bein' clever," he says, "I'm a professor from Harvard! Where d'ye get that stuff?"

"It's a gift!" I says. "What are you doin' here this hour of the day?"

"Hurry up and git through eatin'," he says, "I want you to take a ride with me."

"What have you been pinched for?" I says.

"Will you leave him be?" butts in the wife. "Don't mind him, Alex, he'll go with you. Where are you going?"

"Up to Runyon Q. Sampson's to sell him a Gaflooey roadster," says Alex. "I got the car right outside now. Just wait till you git a look at it, you'll be crazy to buy one yourself!"

"You said it!" I tells him, puttin' on my coat. "I certainly would be crazy if I bought one of them! Who's gonna drive this up there?"

"I got a mechanic from the shop," says Alex. "A feller which knows so much about automobiles that he could take a pair of pliers and a lug wrench and go clear to Frisco with nothin' else!"

"Not even a car, eh?" I says. "*Some* mechanic!"

"Be still!" says the wife. "Well, Alex, I certainly hope you have all kinds of luck. Let me know how you make out, will you?"

"Sure!" I tells her. "Call up police headquarters in about an hour and you'll prob'ly be able to get all the details, right off the blotter."

We go outside and there's the Gaflooey chummy roadster leanin' right up against the curb. It looked like it might be a regular automobile when it grew up, but just then it seemed like it had been snatched from the cradle before its features was fully formed. Two of them roadsters would of made a nice pair of roller skates and the expense for tires must of been practically nothin', because the ones that was on it looked like a set of washers. The body was painted yellah and the trimmin's was in Alice blue and catsup red.

In the front seat is this guy which Alex claimed was the world's greatest mechanic. You could see that at a glance anyhow, because he was dressed in a pair of overalls that had lasted him ever since he first broke into the automobile game and he carried about three quarts of medium oil on his face and hands.

"Well," says Alex, throwin' out his chest, "what d'ye think old Runyon Q. Sampson will say when he casts his eye over that, eh?"

"You'd only get sore if I told you," I says, "but I'll say this much, Alex. If you can sell him that mechanical toy there on the pretense that it's an automobile, I'm goin' up to-morrow and sell him Grant's Tomb for a paperweight!"

"Git in," pipes Alex, "and stop knockin'!"

"I won't have to knock after we get started—that's if we do," I tells him, forcin' myself into the rear, "the motor will look after that!"

Alex nudges the mechanic.

"This here's my cousin," he tells him. "He ain't a bad feller in spite of that."

He turns around to me, "Joe," he says, "I want you to meet Mister Eddie Worth, the best man on gas engines that ever burnt his hands on an exhaust pipe!"

"Greetin's, Eddie!" I says, shakin' hands with him and gettin' a half pound of grease for nothin'.

"Gimme a cigarette!" answers Eddie. "I been waitin' here an hour for youse guys. The motor is prob'ly all cold now and the starter may gimme an argument."

He gets out and monkeys around the front of the car.

"Ain't it nice and roomy back there?" Alex asks me.

I moved my knees away from my chin so's I could talk.

"Great!" I says. "Only the Gaflooey people is liable to get in trouble on account of them coppin' the design from somebody else."

"What d'ye mean?" he asks me, lookin' puzzled.

"Well," I tells him, "you gotta admit that the seatin' arrangements back here is a dead steal from a can of sardines!"

"Did you ever see anything you couldn't find fault with?" he sneers.

"Yeh," I says. "I once got three nickels in change for a dime."

At this critical moment, the mechanic gets down on his hands and knees in the street and begins to worry the car like a dog with a bone. Then all of a sudden he crawls underneath it and disappears from the public eye. A lot of shippin' clerks, bookkeepers, salesgirls, brokers, lawyers and the like, on their way downtown to their jobs, figures that you can go to work any day, but an auto bein' fixed calls for immediate attention and gets around us in a circle. This seemed to get Alex's goat, but it was huckleberry pie to the mechanic. He crawls out from under, rolls up his sleeves, ruffles his hair, looks over the crowd and rubs his hands together.

"Gimme a cigarette!" he says. "And reach down in that tool box there and hand me up them pliers, a couple of S wrenches, the hammer and a screwdriver!"

The crowd sighs with delight, but Alex leaps off the seat like they was bees in the upholstery.

"What d'ye want all them there tools for?" he yells. "Stop this monkey business, I'm an hour late now! What's the matter with the car?"

The mechanic looks around at the crowd and shakes his head pityin'ly. They give Alex the laugh, and a manicure tells her friend that if she was the mechanic she wouldn't bother with it, but would make Alex fix it himself for gettin' so bold.

"What's the matter with the car?" repeats the mechanic, waggin' his head from side to side with a sarcastic movement. "It's been abused, that's all! I ain't had time to go over it carefully; it'll have to be towed down to the shop where we can git it up on jacks and take it apart. I found a leak in the radiator, the bolts is missin' from the muffler, there's a crack in the rear housin' and the clutch seems to grind a bit."

Alex grits his teeth and grabs hold of the windshield.

"Is that all?" he hisses.

"Well, not *all*, no!" says the mechanic, scratchin' his chin. "They must be a couple of pins sheered off of the differential and the—"

"They ain't no sich a thing!" roars Alex. "This here's a brand new car, right from our factory—you wooden-headed fule! It ain't been run a mile and they ain't a thing the matter with it, not even a scratch on the paint! You was sent up here to drive this car, not to wreck it. You—"

"Hey, don't git to callin' me no wooden-headed fool!" hollers the mechanic, jumpin' around and wavin' the pliers. "That's against the union rules, and you'll get the worst of it if I bring it before the board. They must be some mistake here. I thought you wanted me to look over this boat for your friend here and see what it needed. How'd I know you only wanted me to drive? I ain't no mind-reader, I'm a mechanic and—"

"Shut up!" says Alex; "and drive us out to Tarrytown. As a matter of fact, the car's all right, ain't it?"

"Certainly!" says the mechanic. "Ain't it a new one? Gimme a cigarette and I'll see if I can get this tin can here to roll."

It's just about eighteen miles as the pigeon soars from where we started to Runyon Q. Sampson's country home at Tarrytown, and we fled up there in two hours. This car was a wonder on hills, that is it's a wonder we got up 'em at all. We climbed most of 'em with the emergency brake on so's we wouldn't slip back to the garage, and I figured that the car must of been painted yellah in honor of the motor, which quit like a dog every time the goin' got rough. The mechanic drives us in through the entrance of Sampson's domicile, as we remark at the garage, and then stops for encouragement before goin' further. Alex elects me to go up and notify Sampson that we're all set to show him the Gaflooey chummy roadster, while he and the mechanic stays behind to look over the car and see that everything is workin' fairly perfect. I got as far as the porch and a guy in a drum-major's uneyform without the hat nails me. He was as big as the

Woolworth Buildin' and just as emotional. He looked like what them stage butlers tries to.

"What would you wish?" he asks, friendly as a traffic cop to a taxi-driver.

"Well, if I thought they was any use," I says, "I'd wish I had a million bucks, but as it is, I'd like to see Runyon Q. Sampson, your master."

"Step this way!" he says, startin' to walk ahead.

"I can't step that way!" I says, watchin' him close. "It must be a gift. I'll have to folley you in my own way on account of havin' a blowout in my rubber heels an—"

Just then a little bald-headed guy with one of them short gray mustaches which the wealthy banker wears in the movies, crosses our path and the big feller stops and salutes him.

"Gentleman to see you, sir," he says.

"Hmph!" grunts Runyon Q. Sampson, which is who the little guy was, as the gentle readers has prob'ly guessed. "I can't see any one now. I have an appointment this afternoon to—"

"I guess I'm that appointment," I butts in, "or part of it, anyways. Was you expectin' to look over a Gaflooey chummy roadster?"

"Well, what of it?" he snaps.

"My lord, the carriage awaits!" I says, makin' a bow. "Folley me and you'll go motorin'!"

"Are you the agent?" he asks, as we walk back over the lawn.

"No," I says, "I'm his cousin. He's carryin' me along for luck or somethin'. We also have a mechanic with us in case of fire. Are you fond of automobilin'?"

"Much more so than of conversation!" he barks.

"That stops me!" I says. "I'm dumb from now on. What is it who's this says? Silence is golden, speech is human—ain't it?"

We have reached the car by this time, and Alex steps forward.

"Good morning, Mister Sampson!" he says. "I want to thank you for the company and myself, for volunteering your judgment as to whether our new model chummy roadster is a good car or not."

Sampson walks around it a couple of times, opens the hood, looks at the motor and sniffs.

"It's entirely too small!" he announces. "The body is grotesque, the paint is a horrible color and the chassis seems out of alignment."

"Exactly what I thought you would say!" agrees Alex, noddin' his head like Sampson had raved over the car. "We will make any changes you suggest. After all, you'll be the one to use it and that makes you the one to be pleased. We have custom made suits, shoes and shirts—why not custom made automobiles?"

"Hmph!" grunts Sampson.

"I'll fall," I says, hopin' to break the embarrassin' silence. "Why not?"

"Shut up!" hisses Alex. "Would you allow us to give you a little spin?" he asks.

"Ha, ha!" pipes the mechanic all of a sudden. "That's a hot one, ain't it?" he grins at Sampson. "Sure, old top, we'll give you a spin!" he says, jabbin' the floor board with his feet. "That's if this boiler will roll. Some of you guys will have to give the motor a little spin, if you want to go away from here. She's gone cold on me again! Gimme a cigarette, will you?"

Alex presented him with a glance that would of froze boilin' oil.

"Step right in, Mister Sampson," he says. "We'll run around the roads here and—"

"We'll do nothing of the sort!" snaps Sampson. "I've got to be at my office by three o'clock and you can drive me down there. In that way I'll be wasting no time and I can see what your car can do through traffic as well as on the road."

"Elegant!" says Alex. "Step right in."

Runyon Q. Sampson steps right in and after gettin' a cigarette from me, the mechanic steps on the gas. We run every bit of a hundred yards across the lawn and then all of a sudden the Gaflooey roadster stops deader than Columbus. The mechanic tried everything from blowin' the horn to crawlin' underneath it again, but they was nothin' stirrin'.

"Well," he says to Alex, finally, "there's only one way we can get away from here now!"

"What's that?" asks Alex, bendin' down so's Runyon Q. Sampson won't hear it.

"By freight!" says the mechanic. "It seems to me that one of them rear axles has gone to work and busted on us."

"Listen to me," says Alex. "Get us away from here right away and there's ten dollars extry in it for you!"

"Now you're talkin' sense!" says the mechanic. "Gimme a cigarette."

He grabs up the tool box and hides himself under the car again, while Runyon Q. Sampson begins to fidget around and look at his watch like it was the first one he ever seen.

Twenty minutes passed, folleyed by thirty more, and still this mechanic is under the car, makin' sounds like he was fillin' a rush order for tin pans. Alex is as nervous as a cop makin' his first pinch and our friend Sampson begins sayin' things about the Gaflooey roadster that would never of been used by the builders as testimonials. Finally, Alex whispers to me will I get underneath and see what the world's champion auto mechanic is doin' to while away the time.

I got out and looked under and—Oh, boy!

This bird is layin' on the ground under the car, readin' a dope book on the races! He's got the book in one hand and a hammer in the other and every now and then he reaches back and wallops the dirt pan, without lookin', so's it'll sound like he's fixin' things up.

"What seems to be the trouble?" I asks him.

"I think Dimpled Dan is like money from home in the first race to-day," he says, "provided they—what—what are you doin' here?" he winds up, droppin' the book.

"Git outa there!" I hollers. "If you're a mechanic, I'm Christopher Columbus!"

"What d'ye expect for seventy cents an hour—Edison?" he growls.

Runyon Q. Sampson has took it all in and now he lets out a beller and leaps from the car.

"You infernal idiot!" he bawls at poor Alex. "You've made me miss my appointment. What do you mean by taking up my time with this travesty on an automobile? Why, the thing can't even move! If this is the way it performs when it's fresh from your factory, what can a man expect when it's a few weeks old?"

"Maybe it ain't ripe enough yet," I butts in, hopin' to save the situation. "It does look kinda young, don't it?"

"Silence!" roars Runyon Q. "I wouldn't buy one of your cars if they were selling at three cents a carload! That's final! Don't you dare come up and bother me again. Get this pile of junk off my place here just as fast as you can, or, by the eternal, I'll have you all arrested for trespassing!"

With them few remarks he stamps off across the lawn, bellerin' like a bull.

"Well, Alex," I says, "at last you have hit somethin' in little old New York that you can't do, eh?"

"That old boob gimme a pain anyways!" remarks the mechanic. "What does he know about machinery? Gimme a cigarette!"

Alex sits down on the runnin' board of the Gaflooey chummy roadster and lights a cigar. He puffs away, lookin' off in the air kinda sad and mournful, like he had just been handed a wire readin', "Father has told all. We are lost.—Agnes," or somethin' to that effect. Even though he was a relative of the wife's and had spent every minute since he hit New York confessin' to bein' a world beater, I felt sorry for him! Runyon Q. Sampson was off the Gaflooey people for life, and Alex had fell down on the biggest thing he'd tried yet. I knew how he must of felt about it, so I went over and slapped him on the back.

"Cheer up, Alex," I says. "I know that was a tough one to lose, but a guy can't finish in front all the time! You know you ain't up in dear old Vermont now and this town's much harder to beat than the average. I told you that when you first come here. I knowed it was only a question of time before you'd hit the bumps—everybody does sooner or later in New York—and then you—"

43

Alex gets up and throws away the cigar.

"All I hope," he says. "All I hope is that the one they deliver to him works all right!"

"Deliver to who?" I says.

"Runyon Q. Sampson!" he comes back. "I come up here to sell that feller a Gaflooey chummy roadster and that's what I'm a goin' to dew! I'll have his check before the end of the week. I don't know how I'm gonna do it now, but in some way this here sale is gonna occur, you can gamble on that! D'ye think a little thing like this can discourage me? Why if the car had exploded and blowed us all up in the air while we was sittin' in it, I would of sold Sampson the speedometer for a watch before we had hit the ground again!" He turns around on the mechanic and rolls up his sleeves. "The faster you git away from here, the longer you'll live!" he snarls. "What art was you follerin' before you took up automobiles?"

"Well, to be on the level with you," says the mechanic, "I was second man in a cigar store on Twenty-third Street. I got fired because me and the cash register could never agree on the day's receipts. I seen an ad for a mechanic at the Gaflooey service station and I got took on there as a helper. A feller has got to do something don't he? Gimme a cigarette."

Alex makes a dash for him, but I hold him back.

"Fade!" I warns him. "You're gettin' away with murder as it is, and if I let this bird go they's no tellin' what'll happen to you!"

"What do I get for my mornin's work, heh?" he hollers.

"You're gettin' immunity!" I says. "Beat it!"

"All right!" he snarls. "I oughta knowed I'd only get the worst of it goin' out on a job with a coupla boobs like you guys. This feller claims he's a salesman, hey? Well, I'll lay the world eight to five he couldn't sell ice cream sodas in Hades! Gimme a ciga—"

Alex throws the tool box at him, and he blows.

While we're standin' there tryin' to figure out some way to get this chummy roadster to make good, a guy steps out from behind a hedge and joins our little party. He had just about passed the votin' age and he wore a raincoat with one of them cute little belts around it, a dare-devil soft hat and carried a suitcase. His feet dragged like they wasn't used to such heavy exercise as walkin' and he steps in front of us with a cigarette droopin' outa the corner of his mouth.

"Pardon me," he yawns. "Are you having some difficulty with the car?"

"Oh, fluently!" I says. "You must be a fortune teller. Some difficulty is right! We been attemptin' to get away from here all mornin' and it's the same as makin' the Russians think the Czar was a good feller—there's nothin' doin'. I don't think the motor is tryin' and—"

He sets down the suitcase and yawns some more.

"I know something about autos," he says. "Have a couple of my own and occasionally I have to fuss around 'em a bit. Do you mind if I look at the motor?"

"We'd just love it!" I says. "Go to it."

He opens the hood, yawns a coupla times and monkeys around for a minute.

"Try her now," he says.

Alex gets in and pushes a button with his foot.

I don't know what this handsome stranger did, but whatever else it was, it was a success, because the motor immediately begins to tear holes in the peace and quiet of the surroundin' country.

"She'll be all right as soon as she warms up now," says our savior. "The gas was disconnected—coupling jolted off evidently—and one of the cylinders was missing. Must have given you trouble on hills, what?" he yawns some more. "Nice little bus," he says, "and, now, I wonder if you'd do a favor for me?"

"I only got four bucks on me," I says, "but you're welcome to that if you can use it."

He grins.

"It isn't money," he says. "It's something more important than that."

"Fudge!" says Alex. "There ain't no sich thing in this town!"

"Yes there is!" says the newcomer, steppin' back to a hedge, "and here it is!"

With that, out steps the Venus de Milo wearin' both arms and a set of scenery that must of enabled some Fifth Avenue store to move over to Easy Street. She looked like what the press agents claim is in the chorus of every musical comedy that hits Broadway and she's wearin' enough diamonds to have keep the Alleys in tooth powder. After I had got over bein' dazzled by the first look, I give her the East and West again and recognize her. She's nothin' less than Margot Meringue, the big movie star.

"I'm Arnold Sampson," says the young feller, "and this is Mrs. Arnold Sampson. My wife was formerly—"

"I know," I butts in, "I seen her the week before last with the missus in Marvelous Margot's Mistake. She was vampirin' around and—"

"How did you like me?" smiles Margot.

"Well," I says, "we seen the pitcher three times runnin'—is that good enough?"

"We have just been married," goes on Arnold, throwin' out what chest he had with him.

"Congratulations!" pipes Alex, shakin' his hand.

"Pretty soft!" I says, doin' the same.

"I saw you and father in the car here," explains Arnold, "and as you appear to be friends of his, I wonder if you'd come up to the house with us? Father is less liable to make a scene, if there is some one else present. You see, he doesn't know that we're married as yet."

Alex suddenly looks interested and nudges me to keep quiet.

"I can see the whole thing in a nutshell," he says. "Your father objects to you—oh—now—marryin' an actress, heh?"

"No," yawns Arnold. "In this case the traditional is reversed. My father objects to the actress marrying me!" he bows to Margot. "He is personally quite fond of my wife and his objection is based solely upon his own unflattering opinion of me. He declares I'll never be able to support Mrs. Sampson in the manner she is accustomed to living, as her income is something like fifty thousand a year. Father allows me a bare five thousand and he refuses to increase it until I go to work in his office, or something equally as silly. Can you imagine anything more idiotic than that? Dad is worth millions and he expects me to work!"

"What an inhuman parent!" says Alex. "What have you got against work?"

"My dear fellow," says Arnold, "I don't really know. I don't seem able to get enthusiastic about it—that's all. I wouldn't mind going down to Dad's office and toying with an adding machine or driving nails in packing cases, but I'm sure I'd fall asleep on the job, or something idiotic like that! You might say I lack the urge," he yawns and grins. "I guess I wasn't built to hustle. I haven't got the pep, as we used to say at—"

"Listen!" butts in Alex, his eyes beginnin' to glitter. "You was built the same as anybody else, only thinner. I know what's the matter with you—c'mere, I'll show you!" He takes Arnold by the arm and leads him over to the Gaflooey chummy roadster. "D'ye see that automobile there?" he says. "Look at it. What is it—nothin' but a pile of metal and wood! It can't talk, it can't think—but it's got a little button down there in the dash and when you push it, that car will keep on runnin' till the gasoline gives out or it hits a tree! That button's called a self-commencer and that's what you need! Ain't there no buttons up in your head that you can push and get yourself goin'? Is that pile of metal better than you? You can go down now and take a job where you won't get your hands dirty, but if your Dad hadn't been a self-starter fifty years ago, *you'd* be callin' a Wop foreman 'Boss' to-day and likin' it!"

Arnold stops yawnin' and looks interested, where he don't look mad. Margot nods her head and puts her hand on his arm.

"Arnold dear," she says, "he's right! It's time you did try to do something, especially now. I don't want to lecture you, dear, but—"

"I don't know whether he's right or not," says Arnold, "but I do know that extraordinary speech of his has me thinking. Also, it sounded great to me and there's no reason why it shouldn't sound just as great to Dad! He loves that sort of thing and I'm going up and repeat it, word for word! I'm going to tell him we're married and that I'll start to work for him whenever he likes. I can try it, anyhow!"

Margot looks at Alex like she would kiss him if it wasn't for the looks of the thing, and Alex whispers in my ear that the Gaflooey roadster is as good as sold. We all got in it—it was runnin' like a watch now—and roll up to the house. The newly-weds goes inside, while me and Alex stays out on the porch, and in about half an hour they come out again, bringin' old Runyon Q. Sampson with 'em. The old gent walks over to Alex and holds out his hand.

"My boy," he says, "I want to thank you for what you've done to this cub of mine. I don't know what you told him, but he's a different person from the time I saw him last. He sounds like a real man, now! I'm going to do something for you in return. I won't buy one of these infernal cars of yours, wouldn't have it for a gift! But, if you'll tell me what your commission on the sale would have amounted to, I'll write you a check for that figure."

Margot looks at Alex, and then she looks at the car.

"Why, I think its a perfect dear!" she says, "and those colors real harmony itself!"

Alex bounces forward, his eyes glitterin' again.

"We were thinkin' of callin' this model the Margot Meringue," he says, "and—"

"Come, come!" interrupts old Runyon Q., "let's straighten this matter up." He takes out his check book and fountain pen. "I want to take you children down to Tiffany's and have Margot pick out a suitable wedding gift. We have—"

"May I have anything I want?" asks Margot, kinda innocent.

"Of course you can!" beams the old boy, pinchin' her cheek.

"Then buy me a Gaflooey chummy roadster!" she says. "I think this one is a perfect love of a car!"

Oh, boy!

Alex tries to look unconcerned, but he couldn't help droppin' his hat. The old man coughs and gets red in the face, but he was game.

"All right!" he snorts at Alex. "You win. You can say you're the only man that ever got the best of Runyon Q. Sampson! What's the amount?"

I went into the office of the Gaflooey Company with Alex when he went back and the president is waitin' for him with blood in his eye.

"You needn't begin your excuses!" he says to Alex. "The mechanic has told me how you made a mess of everything and Sampson refused to buy the car. I didn't think they made any ten-thousand-a-year-men up in Vermont when I hired you, but I took a chance. New York's too big for you fellows; I guess you were only a flash in the pan! Just think what it would have meant had you sold the car to old Sampson! Why, the advertising alone would—"

"I guess you're right about me bein' a flash in the pan," butts in Alex, "but I found another pan! I don't know whether this is any good for advertisin' or not, but I sold that chummy roadster to Sampson and he has give it to his daughter-in-law for a weddin' gift."

The president jumps from his chair, very light for a man of his heft.

"Great!" he hollers, "great!" He looks at Sampson's check which Alex hands over. "I knew you'd do it! I saw you had the stuff in you the minute you first walked in this office. That's the place to get first string men—right from the country, and Vermont has furnished more than her share. They told me you'd fall down because New York was too big for you, but I knew different. They can't fool me when it comes to judging men! I'll get our advertising men right to work on this copy, and we'll hit the morning papers with it. This is great! Now if Sampson's daughter-in-law was only in the public eye, know what I mean, this would be wonderful! We've had a man after Margot Meringue for a month, but she's away somewhere. You probably won't know her; she's a big movie star and we'd *give* her a car if she'd only endorse it. Why, if we landed her—"

"That's who Sampson give the car to," says Alex. "His son and her just got wed and he give her the Gaflooey roadster for a weddin' gift. How about that New York manager job—do I get it?"

"Do you get it!" shrieks the president. "Why, say—you're *it*, right now!"

"That's fine!" says Alex. "I'll take the job the day after to-morrow!"

"I see!" says the president, breakin' his neck tryin' to make himself a good fellah. "You want a day off after your labors, eh?"

"No!" says Alex, "I got to go out and see Sampson again to-morrow, because havin' give this roadster to his daughter-in-law, naturally he'll need one for hisself now!"

CHAPTER III

PLAY YOUR ACE!

This here combination that opens the door to success is a funny thing—everybody's lookin' for it and everybody's got it! Some guys knows just where to put their hands on it when they get the big chance to crack the safe of fame and as a result they become boss bankers or boss bricklayers—either of which is a trick and hard to do. Other guys forget the first three numbers or somethin' and never get better than John Smiths in the telephone book of life.

It takes speed to get a baseball from the pitcher to the catcher, but it's *control* that puts the pill over the plate, which may be the answer to why John D. Rockefeller ain't payin' *you* rent and you got your first time to be elected president of anything, from the dear old U. S. A. to the Red Carnation Social Club. Instead of sittin' around knockin' winners every time the papers print a new one, give yourself the once over and see if you can find out what *your* trick is. You may only be able to wiggle your left ear funnier than anybody on the block—Great! *Cash on it!* It's a cinch you can do *somethin'*, and once you find out what that somethin' is, the rest is as easy as fallin' off Pike's Peak!

No—easier! Because you gotta climb Pike's Peak before you can fall off. You may be a guy like Hector Sells, which started life with a straight flush, and played it like it was a pair of deuces. If somebody hadn't peeped over his shoulder, seen what he held and played it for him, Hector would still be thinkin' that the only guy in the world drawin' over twenty bucks a week was J. P. Morgan. As it is, Hector has $2.75 right now for every wave in the ocean, and when you go to see him, you become acquainted with all the office boys in the world.

Here's the answer.

One night after dinner the wife and I are provin' to each other that the road of true love is rough and full of detours, when they's a ring at the bell. We practised self-denial and laid off scrappin' long enough for friend wife to open the door. I made a bet with myself and win easy. In comes Alex.

"Huh!" he says. "Is they an argument goin' on here again?"

"You said it!" I tells him. "Come on in, you're just in time. We'll make it three-handed!"

"I don't know why you got married when you're always quarrelin'," he says, sittin' down.

"That ain't all you don't know!" I says.

"Kindly lay off my cousin," says the wife. "They ain't no use in showin' the world that I have married a brute!"

With that she presses four dollars' worth of Irish lace against her eyes and develops a cold in the head. So the same as usual, I went over and patted her on the shoulder which was shakin' the most.

"You win, honey!" I says, with a dollar's worth of vaseline on every word. "I'll never speak another harsh word to you or Alex again. The next time I feel sarcastic, I'll go out in the kitchen and have some words with the cat. Everybody in the apartment house knows what I think of *you*, and I must be *wild* over Alex or he'd never be in this flat a second time. If—"

"Never mind the salve!" cuts in the wife. "You'd talk your way out of pneumonia!"

But they was a smile went with that—the same giggle that used to make 'em fight for standin' room in the Winter Garden. So we was all happy and carefree again, with the exception of Alex.

"You're too easy with him!" he growls to the wife, disappointed because peace had come. "If you'd punish him, he'd be a better husband."

"She does punish me somethin' cruel!" I says. "By invitin' *you* up every day!"

And then of course all bets was off and we all went over the top again!

In about an hour, the people in the next flat had enough, and mentioned the fact to the landlord. He let us in on it by way of the phone, and all was quiet along the Hudson again.

"I come up here to-night to tell you somethin'," says Alex.

"They's always the United States mail," I says.

"I ain't talkin' to you, I'm speakin' to Cousin Alice!" snarls Alex.

"She can read too!" I says.

"I been thinkin' this here thing over for weeks," he goes on, turnin' his chair so's I can get a good view of his back, "and I made up my mind to-day to go ahead with it."

"What is it, Alex?" asks the wife, all excited. "I know it's goin' to be somethin' wonderful!"

"You ain't gonna tell me you're gonna stop eatin' here, are you?" I says. "Because if you are, I'm gonna beat it! I heard tell of guys dyin' of joy and I ain't takin' no chances!"

"The whole trouble with you," says Alex, "is a simple case of jealousy. You was born and brung up in this rube burg called New York and the best you could do in thirty-five years was to get yourself foreman of a baseball team! I—"

"Yeh!" I butts in. "I fell down the same as Caruso. All he can do is sing!"

"I come here from Vermont," goes on Alex, now on his favorite subject, "and right off the reel I get me a ten thousand a year job, not countin' commissions, sellin' autos. Now I claim that what *I* did in New York can be done by anybody—and I'm here to prove it! It's just as easy to be a roarin' success in New York as it is in Paterson, N. J.—and just as hard! There's many a Charlie Chaplin sellin' groceries and many a Theodore Roosevelt carryin' bricks! In their off hours and in the privacy of their homes, them fellers is doin' for *nothin'*, what Chaplin, Roosevelt, Dempsey and so forth got *paid off* on! If a man's a gambler, for instance, and he bets on a race horse, the chances are he stays up all night lookin' up the past performances of that horse and seein' just what he can do under all conditions. He studies how the horse finished on a muddy track and where he come in when the track was fast. He makes note of what the horse did under different weights and different jockeys. He watches what it does against certain other horses. Then when he thinks everything is favorable, he bets his money! He—"

"Look here, Alex!" I butts in. "Did you come all the way up here to-night to lay me on a horse race?"

"No!" he snorts, in disgust, "I come up here to lay you on *yourself*! If this same man that studies the dope before he bets on a horse, would study the dope on *himself* with the same attention to detail, before he enters the handicap of life—he'd be a winner! He wouldn't have to bet on no horses or nothin' else, because he'd be his own best bet! He'd find out what his particular ace was and play it to the limit every time! Instead of that, the average feller spends his time sittin' in the greatest game in the world—life—drawin' five cards every time and waitin' for the royal flush to be dealt him pat. He—"

"My goodness, Alex!" remarks the wife, "I didn't know you was a gambler. Where did you learn all those poker terms?"

"He once claimed casino was vicious, too!" I says.

Alex gets up and reaches for his hat.

"There ain't no use talkin' to people which has checked their brains with the hat boy!" he says. "But before I go, I wanna tell you this. Every man has got the key to his own success buried in him somewhere, and I'll bet I can take the champion dub of any given precinct and make him a winner the minute I find out where he hid *his!*"

"Let's go to the movies, instead of fightin' like cats and dogs," remarks the wife, puttin' on her handbag.

"Yes!" sneers Alex, "let's go to the movies and knock the leadin' man because he's gettin' $30,000 a year, and let's explain to each other how he's gettin' away with murder and ain't got a thing but his looks. That's much better than sittin' down and figurin' how we can make the same amount of money, if we—"

"Look here, Alex!" I interrupts, gettin' a trifle peeved. "You took me for eight hundred berries when you first invaded New York and, sucker like, I'm lookin' for a come-back. Are you on the level with that stuff about you bein' able to put *anybody* over if you get in their corner?"

"Am I on the level with it?" he says. "Why, say!—I'm goin' in the *business* of makin' successes outa dubs! I'm gonna take 'em one by one, put 'em over and charge a reasonable percentage for my work. I'm sick and tired of the automobile game and I'm gonna incorporate myself as Alex Hanley, S. D."

"What's the S. D. for?" I asks. "South Dakota?"

"No—Success Developer!" he says. "I ain't selfish—I put myself over and now I'm gonna put 'em *all* over! At the same time, as I say, I'll charge a reasonable sum for my work. Why this is bigger business than Wall Street, makin' men instead of breakin' 'em and—"

"Stop talkin' for a second, Alex," I says, "and get a new sensation! I got an idea of what that reasonable charge of yours will be, that's provided your scheme works, which it prob'ly won't. If you cause a guy to make himself twenty dollars, your fee won't exceed a hundred and fifty! You're as liberal with money as Grant's Tomb is with advice. But if you're on the level with this, I'll bet you a thousand bucks, American money, to five hundred of the same coinage, that you'll flop like a seal on your first try. They's only one thing you gotta do!"

"What is it?" he asks. He was thinkin' of them thousand bucks and his eyes sparkled till you could of hocked 'em anywheres for five hundred apiece.

"You gotta let *me* pick the first victim!" I says.

"Not to change the subject," remarks the wife to me, "if you got a thousand dollars for purposes of bettin', they's a ring in Tiffany's window which will come here to-morrow escorted by a C.O.D. bill. The price and one thousand dollars is the same."

"Do you think I print this money myself?" I hollers.

"I would of married you long ago if I did!" she says, smilin' sweetly.

"Think of a man mean enough to argue about money with his lovin' wife!" sneers Alex.

"If *you* was married," I says, "your wife would think they had stopped the circulation of all money, with the exception of nickels!"

"Ha! Ha!" he sneers, like a movie villain. "I just give Eve Rossiter an engagement ring that can be *pawned* for eight hundred men!"

"I think you're four flushin'," I hollers, gettin' warmed up, "but you can't hang nothin' on me! You go down to Tiffany's, honey," I tells the wife, "and get that thousand buck ring—but put up a battle for it at $750!"

The wife pulls her million-dollar smile and gimme a chaste salute, as the guy says, on the forehead. Then she opens her sea-goin' handbag and takes somethin' out.

"Here it is, dear!" she says, with the giggle that made me a married man, "I knowed you'd fall, so I got it this morning! It was only $987. Ain't I the great little buyer?"

Oh, boy!

"Well," I says to Alex, "it seems to be the open season for takin' me. Does that bet go?"

"It does!" he says, rubbin' his hands together like a crap shooter.

"And I produce the first candidate for fame and fortune?"

"Bring him on!" he grins, winkin' at the wife—a thing he knows I loathe.

We shook hands on it and I went out into the kitchen to laugh it over with the cat. I'm a soft-hearted boob and I hate to take a sucker, at that. But accordin' to my dope, that dough of friend Alex's was the same as in the bank in my name!

Now the bird I had in mind to make me win this bet from Alex was a pitcher I had on the payroll who's name was Hector Sells. He would of been just as rotten a ball player if his name had been First Base, Center Field or Short Stop. He could do everything in the world with a baseball, with the slight exception of gettin' it over the plate, and, when he pitched, his main difficulty was keepin' the pill outa left field. In the seven years he had been stealin' wages from my club his twirlin' percentage read like the thermometer in Alaska and when he come to bat, as far as he ever found out, first base was in Berlin. I put him on the third base coachin' line one afternoon and he tries to send a runner back to second when the batter triples. I tried this guy out at every position on the team and he made so many errors that the official scorers went out and bought addin' machines every time he appeared in the line-up. If they was anything on earth connected with the game of baseball that Hector could do, he never showed it to me, and puttin' a uneyform on him was the same as givin' a blind man a pair of opera glasses.

Yet with all this, that guy thought he was the greatest baseball player that ever laid hold of a glove. He not only thought it, he *conceded* it.

For the past year, Hector had played out the schedule from the dugout, with the exception of six games he pitched against the Athletics. He lost an even six. I sent him to every flag station in North America where they looked on baseball as a game, and Hector would come back at the end of the season with his suit case jammed full of unconditional releases. Him and pneumonia was just as easy to get rid of as far as I was concerned and we started off every season with Hector in our midst.

Three winters in succession I loaned that guy enough dough to set himself up in business, so's he'd lay off me and watch the pastime from the grandstand. He lost a cigar store shootin' craps, a pool room bettin' with the customers and a delicatessen because he eat all the stock himself. I got him a job on the road sellin' sportin' goods, and the only thing he sold all year was a pitcher's glove at $1.25. He bought that himself.

Now the thing is—why did I keep a guy like that on my club for the lengthy space of seven years? The newspaper birds claimed Hector had seen me murder somebody or somethin', because they says I wouldn't let him in a ball park with a ticket, if he didn't have *somethin'* on me that must be kept from the world at any price. Well, it wasn't nothin' like that—but it was somethin' just as good, as the grocer says. Me and Hector was kids together in the same ward, and when we started out to dumfound the world, he had a bankroll which his beloved father left him and I had nothin' but freckles. I practically lived off that guy till me and real money became well acquainted, so I couldn't see him get the worst of it now. It would of broke his heart if he ever got shoved outa organized baseball—he was a maniac about the game! So Hector drawed his dough every season, come what may—and at that I was doin' no more than he did for me.

I managed to keep him busy in some way about the park—always with a uneyform on—and now and then I let him pitch an innin' when we had the game locked away in the safe deposit vault. In all the seven years, he never missed a single day showin' up at the park and he was the rottenest ball player that ever stood under a shower. Them was Hector's two records!

Well, I dragged Alex out to the ball park the next day and pointed out Hector to him. We was playin' St. Looey and along around the sixth innin' we had the game sewed up so tight that they couldn't of won it in a raffle. I took out Harmon and sent Hector in to pitch.

"Gaze over this bird carefully, Alex!" I says, "because he's the baby you're gonna pay off on! I claim you are now peerin' at the champion dub of the world. If you can make a winner outa him or discover what he has failed to develop that would make him one, I'll not only pay my end of our bet with a grin, but I'll throw in a weddin' chest of silver for you and Eve Rossiter!"

"Write that down!" says Alex; "and sign your full name to it!"

"You don't think I'd welsh on you, do you?" I says, gettin' sore.

"I don't know if they's enough ink in this or not," he answers, handin' me a fountain pen. "Write it on the back of this card."

When the crowd sees Hector strollin' out to the box, they give him his usual reception, which was the same as the Kaiser would have got if he'd walked down Broadway along in April, 1917. The first guy up for St. Looey hit a roller through the box and Hector stood on his left shoulder tryin' to pick it up. The runner only got as far as second before Hector arose. The next guy put a neat round hole in the right field fence, makin' it two runs. Well, before it was three out they had got four more and the only guy connected with the St. Looey team that didn't get a hit was the owner. They only quit slammin' the pill because they had batted themselves sick and could no longer stagger up to the plate.

Hector comes to bat in the next innin' with the bases as full as a miner on pay night. He lets two go by, right in the slot, and he fell down skinnin' his nose, swingin' at the next for the third and last strike.

I removed him by hand and sent in a ball player to pitch the rest of the game.

"Well, Alex," I says on the way home, "what do you think of your patient?"

"Is he as bad as that every day?" he asks me.

"No," I says. "He was Ty Cobb and Walter Johnson to-day, alongside of what he usually is!"

"Hmmph!" grunts Alex. "I can see he ain't a ball player, anyway."

"You been readin' 'Sherlock Holmes,'" I says.

"Baseball ain't everything!" declares Alex, rubbin' his nose. "And the point we have to consider is—what *can* he do?"

"That's easy!" I says. "How much is seven from seven?"

"Why—nothin'," says Alex.

"That's Hector!" I says.

With that I told him Hector's pedigree from the time he crossed my path when an infant, to date. I left out nothin' and laid it on good and thick. I explained how Hector had been the world's most consistent failure from the time he had been introduced as "It's a boy!" up to the time of writin' and when I got all through, Alex grins like a wolf.

"A most promisin' case!" he says. "This here's somethin' that's gonna put me on my mettle, right at the start. The tougher a thing looks, the more appetizin' it strikes me! Now I'll take it for granted that this man's got no *strong* points. All right—that's nothin' but a detail! You've told me a lot of hard things about him, but you ain't said he ain't human—and if he's human he's got a *weakness*! A well-developed weakness in a man has often been turned into glitterin' gold. Does he drink?"

"Let's save time," I says. "Hector don't know whether whiskey and beer is drinks, or the battery for to-day's game. He couldn't tell you offhand whether tobacco was a thing to chew and smoke or the latest fox trot. The only woman he ever met twice was his mother, and he thinks sayin' 'Darnation!' in earnest is the same as homocide. His only love is baseball and his only weakness is his stomach!"

"Aha!" says Alex. "I knew we'd get at it! He's fond of food, eh?"

"Fond of it?" I says. "Why, this guy can do more things with a steak than Edison can do with a pint of electricity! He took me to a dinner he cooked himself one night and the only thing I recognized on the table was the water. Everything was fixed up after his own recipes and at the drop of a hat he can tell you how many of them calories and proteins they is in a pea!"

"That's enough!" hollers Alex. "He's as good as over right now! He simply picked the wrong trade when he took up baseball, and I'll get him a job as chef in one of the famous hotels so—"

"Don't make me laugh!" I cuts him off. "Would I of bet you, if it was as easy as that? They ain't a chance on earth—I thought of that years ago. Hector wouldn't boil water for money—he only cooks that stuff up for himself. He—"

"A true artist, eh?" says Alex, kinda thoughtful. "That makes it all the better! Bring him up for dinner to-morrow night and let me study him. In a week I'll collect that little bet from you and then I'll be ready to take on the next case."

"You certainly stand well with yourself, don't you?" I sneers. "Well, lemme give you a little tip. Don't try to get that bird to give up baseball, because they ain't a Chinaman's chance of that! The only chance you got is to put him over as a ball player, and if *you* can do *that*, I can sell electric fans to the Esquimaux!"

"Bring him up to-morrow night," says Alex, grinnin' like a wolf. "This looks like a cinch to me!"

I went to Hector in the clubhouse the next afternoon. He had had a hard day playin' the White Sox—from the bench.

"Where are you goin' to-night?" I asks him.

He flushes up a bit.

"Well, Mac," he says, "I have finally found a joint where they know how to cook 'em without abusin' 'em and I was figurin' on goin' there first, so—"

"Cook what?" I butts in.

"Alligator pears!" he says. "Y'know they is a lot of nourishment in them babies when they're properly prepared and—"

"You'll be around at that beanery *to-morrow* night!" I shuts him off. "To-night you're comin' up and have dinner with me."

He gets one shade redder.

"Why," he stammers, "Ahumph! That—er—that's terrible fine of you, Mac, but on the level, I—y'know this place is the only one in New York where they can cook them things and I'm a hound after them! I—"

"Come on!" I says. "We're gonna give the subway a play. The wife's expectin' you and I got a friend that's crazy to meet you. Are you gonna throw me down?"

He backs away and ruffles his hair.

"Mac," he says, "I'll have dinner with you to-night on one condition!"

"Shoot!" I says.

"Well, Mac," he tells me, "they ain't no doubt in my mind that your wife is some cook, but if I'm gonna eat this stuff—I—well, I demand the privilege of cookin' it!"

"Where d'ye get that stuff?" I says. "Why—"

"Lemme do this, Mac," he says, "and you'll never regret it. I can hang it on any chef in New York for money and you'll eat the greatest meal you ever got outside of in your life!"

Well, this was new stuff to me, but I figured I was gonna get five hundred bucks outa it by way of Alex, so I fell.

"All right!" I says. "Come up and cook your head off. I'm game! But if you're as good a cook as you are a ball player, I can see where me and the wife suspends friendly relations for about a year!"

Alex is already on hand when we get to the house and I introduced him to Hector.

"Howdy!" he says. "I seen you pitch the other day and I must say it was a treat! The support they give you was brutal or you'd of shut them other fellers out with ease."

"You know it!" says Hector. "If they's any one thing I can do, it's play baseball. That's my dish!"

The wife horns in.

"I'm so glad to meet you, Mister Sells," she says, givin' Hector the old oil. "My husband talks of nothin' but you night and day!"

Which was true—only not the way she meant it.

"That's fine!" says Hector. "Me and Mac has been friends since they burnt Rome. Where's the kitchen?"

I showed him, and the wife shakes her head as much as to say, "Another rummy, eh?" I steered Hector over to the ice box and told him to go ahead and run wild. When I come out, Alex is featurin' his famous grin, and I gotta show the wife my breath. In about ten minutes the kitchen door opens and Hector's head pops out. His hands is full of flour and so's his suit for that matter, but his face is all lit up like Coney Island.

"I don't wanna be no bother, Mrs. Mac," he pipes, "but could a man get a apron around here?"

We got him inside of some gingham, and he disappeared into the kitchen again.

"Where d'ye get them birds?" says the wife, noddin' after him.

"Sssh!" says Alex. "That feller there is gonna make us all rich before the month is over! We'll have more money than we can count and—"

"Oh, won't that be grand!" says the wife, who'd believe Alex if he told her Missouri started the war. "Then I can have everything I want."

"I thought *that* happened when you got *me*," I says.

"Still," she sighs, payin' me no attention as usual, "money ain't everything."

"No," says Alex, "but it'll get it!"

"We always was used to money," goes on the wife, gettin' kinda doped under the influence of the sweet and savory odors which was comin' from the kitchen. "You know, Alex, that our family was connected with the best people in Vermont."

"They ain't got a thing on a telephone operator," I says. "They get connected with the best people in the United States every day!"

I don't get a tumble from either of them.

"There was Great-uncle Ed," proceeds the wife, kinda dreamy. "If he hadn't died so sudden, he'd of been worth a million."

I tried my luck again.

"That's the one that turned out to be a carbolic acid fiend, ain't it?" I says.

At this point, the greatest meal that ever played a date at our flat, come outa the kitchen escorted by Hector. One whiff of that layout and the greatest chef in the world would of gone out and bought a revolver. Hector is nothin' but smiles.

"Give this a whirl!" he says. "And lemme know what you think of it. I didn't have much to work with—only lamb chops, vegetables and the like, but I did what I could."

Oh, boy!—that was *some* feed! Conversation lagged a bit for about half a hour, while we fell to and demolished this stuff, and Hector swells up like a human yeast cake under the kind words that come his way. Finally, we had to quit eatin' for lack of further accommodations and the wife tells Hector that they ain't no doubt about it, as a cook he wins the garage.

"Oh, that's nothin'," he says; gettin' an attack of modesty. "I'm kinda fussy about my food and I been figurin' out different ways of cookin' up stuff to get the best outa it, for years. That's the only amusement I got. I ain't so much as a cook, but you oughta see me play ball, heh, Mac?"

The old glitter comes into Alex's eyes.

"I seen you play ball, Mister Sells," he says, "and you are a knockout! But what you just said about food interests me more. I'm kinda odd regardin' vittles myself and what I seen in the paper to-day has got me worried sick."

"What was that?" says Hector.

"Well," says Alex, "there's gonna be a fearful shortage of all kinds of meats and vegetables, because all the available food in the U. S. is about to be seized for the army. This time next year we'll all prob'ly be livin' on bread and water and lucky to get it!"

Hector gets as white as precipitated chalk.

"You don't mean it!" he gasps, gettin' half outa his chair.

"It's a fact," says Alex. "I was only readin' it this mornin'."

I thought Hector was gonna fall dead at our feet.

"But—but what am *I* gonna do?" he says, kinda dazed.

"What are *you* gonna do?" I sneers. "What are we *all* gonna do?"

"You don't get me!" he says. "It's all well enough for you guys which can eat common ordinary food like ham and eggs and steaks and chops, but I can't *go* that stuff! All the time I ain't out at the ball park I'm experimentin' with different kinds of stuff to eat, and if they go to work and shut off all them rare vegetables and so forth on me—well, I don't eat, that's all!"

He gets up and reaches for his hat.

"Well," says Alex, "I can see that you and me is pretty much alike. I can't eat porterhouse steaks and French lamb chops as a steady diet, either! My stomach craves them rare dishes the same as yours does, and it sure looks like you and me is gonna starve to death when this food conservation thing goes through!"

Hector slaps his hands together and squares his jaw.

"*I* ain't gonna starve!" he says. "They has got to be 1,500 calories and a amount of proteins in proportion go into my system every day. Not only that, its gotta be in a tasty form! I'm gonna go home and figure this thing out so's I'll be took care of when the government grabs off all the food supplies. They must be somethin' a man can do! Good night, folks—and thanks for the use of the kitchen."

With that he blows.

"I think he's a nut!" remarks the wife, when the hall door bangs.

"Leave him be!" says Alex, rubbin' his hands together, a habit that gets my goat. "I got him started now and—"

"Say!" I says. "I didn't see nothin' in no paper about the government gonna seize all the eats. I think you was kiddin' Hector, myself!"

"You didn't see the Civil War, either, did you?" says Alex. "I suppose you don't believe that, eh? I told you I was gonna put this feller over and if you'll leave me be, I will! I told you every man had an ace buried somewhere, didn't I? Well, Hector's ace is his mad infatuation for his stomach. He's never played it yet, because there's been no reason to do so. As long as he had the money, he could buy the stuff and hash it up in any way his peculiar tastes desired. Once he thinks he *can't* do that, he'll put all he's got under his hat into findin' a way to get all them proteins and calories he wants. I've given him somethin' he never had before—an incentive—and—"

"What do you figure Hector's gonna do to startle the world?" I says.

"Search me!" says Alex, grinnin', "but we'll all get paid off on whatever it is, you can gamble on that!"

The wife sniffs.

"I never heard tell of no man that couldn't eat porterhouse steaks!" she says.

"I seen a lot of them to-day," says Alex, puttin' on his coat.

"Where?" asks the wife.

"I was passin' the Evergreen Cemetery!" says Alex. "Good night, all!"

The next day, Hector comes to me before the game and you never seen such a change in a guy in your life! He looked like he hadn't slept a wink since they buried Washington and he's as nervous as a steam drill.

"Mac," he says, "I wanna ask two favors off of you, the first I asked in a long while."

"Shoot, Hector!" I tells him. "You know I can deny you nothin'."

"I want a week off and the loan of five hundred bucks," he says.

"I'll tell you," I says. "Take *two* weeks off and forget about the five hundred, heh?"

"No, Mac—I gotta have the dough!" he says. "With what I got saved up, I figure it'll be ample."

"Ample for what?" I asks.

"I can't tell no man nothin' about it now," he answers, "but when I come back from my vacation, I'll let you in on it. I don't like to say this, Mac—but when I was slippin' it to you, I never asked whether you wanted it to get a hair cut with or to try and put Wall Street on the bum. If—"

"That's enough!" I cuts him off, takin' out the roll. "Here you are, Hector—and if you want any more they's plenty of it where that come from!"

They was—in the mint.

When Hector had put some distance between himself and the ball park, I begin to think the thing over. If he *did* pull any startlin' stunt, I stood to lose a thousand bucks, not countin' the weddin' gift, to Alex. They was five hundred more I'd invested right then, makin' fifteen hundred in all, which I considered was gettin' into money. For all I knowed, Hector and Alex might be framin' me and they ain't no man livin' who loves bein' a sucker.

I decided right then and there to shoot another nickel on the thing and I called up the Ryan Detective Agency. Mike Ryan had been a friend of me and Hector since we'd been in baseball. I told him the whole layout and asked for a report on the activities of Hector the followin' day, if possible.

It was three days before I seen Ryan's report. He give it to me himself by mouth.

"Say!" he says. "This Hector bird has gone nutty, and I suppose bein' friends of his, you and me had better have him put away where he can't do himself no violence."

"What's he doin'?" I asks.

"Well," says Ryan, "I'll give you the dope since he left the ball park on Monday. The first thing he does is go to the bank and draw out every nickel he's got. Then he moves from the hotel to Cereal Crossin', N. J. This burg casts eleven votes for president every four years and they all work on the same farm. Hector hires a shack away out in the middle of the woods there and, from then on, boxes and crates begins to arrive for him from everywheres but Brazil. I met up with a Secret Service guy who had dropped in to get a line on what kinda bombs Hector was makin' before pinchin' him, and we went

70

through this express stuff durin' the night. The first crate we tackled contained all the glassware in the world of a medical nature. They was bottles, test tubes, bowls and all the stuff usual found in a practical anarchist's workshop. After the first peep, the Secret Service guy wanted to run right over and fit Hector with iron bracelets, but I got him to hold off long enough to look over the rest of the stuff. We went through every box and what d'ye think we found in 'em?"

"I wasn't there," I says. "Tell me."

"Well," says Ryan, grinnin', "when all this stuff was assembled, it would make a first class delicatessen shop and that's all! They was meats, cheese, olive oil, fish, vegetables, pickles, mustard and about fifteen other eatables I never seen or heard tell of before in my life! We busted a lot of it open, lookin' for explosives, but they was all on the level. Why, that bird's got enough stuff down there to keep him in food for the rest of his life!"

I bust out laughin'.

"Ha, ha!" I says. "That's it! The poor fathead went and fell for that bunk Alex handed him and he's gone and laid in that stuff so's he won't starve when the government seizes the food supplies. Can you tie that?"

"I always thought he was a little queer," says Ryan. "Especially when he claims he's a ball player. Let's get him in some nice, private sanitarium somewheres and I'll split the bill with you."

"Leave him alone!" I says. "I'll take care of this myself. If he stays there long enough, I gotta chance to win a piece of money and—"

"All right!" says Ryan. "It ain't no milk outa my coffee, but that bird oughta be under lock and key!"

I could hardly wait to tell Alex about Hector's first step towards success. I rung him up immediately and give him the dope, windin' up by askin' when he'd be ready to pay me off.

"Pay *you* off?" he says. "Save that comedy for Cousin Alice! Just you leave Hector be now; from what you tell me everything's goin' fine and—"

"Goin' fine?" I hollers. "When that poor simp buries himself in Jersey with all the food in the world, do you call that makin' good?"

"Gimme a week!" says Alex. "He said he'd be back then, and if he ain't shown somethin' by that time, you get the check."

"Fair enough!" I says, "and have it certified."

The followin' Monday night, Alex as usual is honorin' me and the wife with his presence at dinner. I was in such good humor that I didn't as much as wince when he calls for another piece of roast beef, makin' an even eight. Hector had failed to appear as advertised and the noted Success Developer had promised to pay me off before he left. They was a ring at the bell and the wife ushers in Hector, ruinin' the night for me!

"I would of reported at the ball park this afternoon like I promised," he says, "only I was in a burg where the only time a train ever stopped there was when one went off the track."

I hardly knowed it was the same Hector which went away the week before. His cheeks was filled out past the legal limit and he had a color that would make an insurance company let him write his own policy. He was Alfred Q. Health—that's all!

"I'm sorry to see you people eatin' the flesh of the cow, roasted in an unscientific manner," he says. "One slab of that is shy just forty-eight calories and they's more proteins in a filetted bean!" He reaches in his pocket and pulls out a little package. "If I can draw up a chair here," he says, "I'll have dinner with you."

"I'll get another plate," says the wife, "and some coffee—"

"Not a thing!" says Hector. "I got mine with me!" With that he unwraps the package and pulls out a thing about the size of a deck of cards. I thought at first it was a razor hone, but Hector bites into it. "Just a glass of water," he says, "though with this a man don't even need that!"

Alex bounces outa his chair and gimme the laugh.

"What's that?" he hollers at Hector.

"That," says Hector, "is the last word in calories, protein and nourishment! It contains each and every juice and sustainin' part of all meats and vegetables known to man, with a little glutein invention of my own combined. It has got it forty ways on all other patent foods, because it's not only nourishin', it's so darned tasty that once you eat it you get the habit, like dope or somethin', and you can't eat anything else! It'll keep forever without ice or preservatives. You don't need liquids with it, it supplies its own juices. It's got a kick like booze and they ain't no alcohol in it. I invented it and I been livin' on it all week. Look me over and—"

"Gimme a bite!" yells Alex.

He grabs this weird lookin' slab of gue and takes a mouthful.

"Oh, lady!" he hollers. "They's just two things I wanna know. What does it cost to make this stuff, and will it stand scientific tests?"

"It costs about two cents a square, roughly speakin'," says Hector, "and it'll stand any test in the world! Three of them things is the day's food for a healthy man and—"

"Will you lend me one for two days?" asks Alex, reachin' for his coat and hat.

Hector pulls out another package.

"Sure!" he says. "I brung one along for you, because you claimed you was the same as me when it come to—"

But Alex and the trick cake of collapsible food was gone!

He showed up at the ball park the end of the week, when Hector was pitchin' against the Red Sox. They got seven runs off him in the second innin' and I was just yankin' him out, when Alex come runnin' down to the dugout.

"Hector!" he hollers. "You're a rich man! No more baseball for yours—why, you can buy a team if you want it and—"

"I thought you claimed you never drank," I says.

"What is your friend ravin' about?" inquires Hector.

Alex answers by shovin' a pink slip of paper into his hands. It was the first check for fifty thousand bucks I ever seen in my life and it was signed by the secretary of the U. S. treasury!

"Why—what kinda stuff is this?" mutters Hector, turnin' the check over and over. "It's made out to me! Why—who—where—who give you—"

"It's all yours!" says Alex, rubbin' his hands together and displayin' all his back teeth. "I took your food to Washington and got the government experts to try it out. They been lookin' for a one-piece ration for the army. They wanted somethin' cheap, palatable and nourishin' that the men would take to. They was after a food that could be easily packed and shipped. They give your food every possible test and accepted it. That fifty thousand is only a first payment—we still got four hundred and fifty thousand comin' for the invention and—"

"My Gawd!" gasps Hector. "They give up all this money for that?"

"Sure!" rattles on Alex. "And all you gotta do is go to the laboratory they're gonna build and show 'em how to make it. We still got four hundred and—"

"Where d'ye get that *we* stuff?" I butts in, seein' my bet with Alex goin' south. "Hector put that over and—"

"And I put *him* over!" says Alex. "I'm the young feller that showed him where *his* ace was! I therefore take one thousand dollars from you, with that weddin' chest of silver, and I'll only charge Hector ten per cent of his profits, as he was my first patient. I—"

"Let's git outa here!" pipes Hector hoarsely. "Think of me with fifty thousand berries and more on the fire!"

Well, we all met at the flat the next afternoon to celebrate. The wife suggested a theatre party with all that goes with it, and I was lookin' over the papers to pick out a good show. Alex is walkin' up and down the room, rubbin' them hands of his together.

"Well, well, well!" he says, slappin' Hector on the back. "To think that the days of slavery is all over! No more reportin' at the ball park every day, no more spring training no more watchin' 'em hit and run. That must be great after seven years of havin' to see it and—"

"Yeh!" mumbles Hector, kinda glum. He's all dressed up like a broken arm and takin' it just as hard.

"Well," I says, "where will we go? We got all the shows in New York to pick from and—"

"Get one that will give Mister Sells a chance to really relax and enjoy himself," says the wife. "Somethin' that will allow him to forget his former—"

"Why not ask Hector?" says Alex. "Where would *you* like to go, Mister Sells?"

Hector gets up and fumbles with his hat.

"Say!" he says. "Let's all go out and see the ball game, heh?"

CHAPTER IV

DON'T GIVE UP THE TIP!

Listen! If you ever wake up some mornin' with an idea for something new—whether it's a soup, a vaudeville act or a religion—and you expect to cash on it, go to the nearest hardware store and ask the guy behind the counter how much he'll take for all the locks in the joint. Take 'em at any price and fasten 'em on the door of the safe where you keep the idea—the same bein' your mouth—and then throw the keys in any good, deep river!

If the inventors of stud poker, movin' pictures, the alligator pear, pneumonia and so forth had gone around talkin' about them things before they got 'em patented they never would of took in a nickel on their idea, but their *friends* would be draggin' down the royalties yet! The minute you tip another guy to your stunt it's yours and his both. He mightn't *mean* to steal your stuff, but he can't help himself. The more he thinks about it, the better he likes it, and it ain't long before he gets believin' it was *his* idea anyways and where do you get off by claimin' you thought of it?

I admit freely that you can't cash on your scheme unless you get it before the world, but the thing is to wait till you got it covered with so many copyrights and patents that not even the James Boys could steal it and then *tell 'em all at once!*

If Edgar Simmons had of did that, he'd be a rich millionaire to-day instead of havin' to cut his winnin's with Alex. Edgar had an idea, and he didn't know what to do with it.

Alex did!

The wife and I is sittin' down to the evenin' meal one night, when the telephone rings. Only one of us got up.

"Hello!" I says.

"Hello!" is the answer. "This is Alex. What would you say to me runnin' up there to supper to-night?"

"Nothin'," I answers. "I see where they was a guy got pinched only last week for swearin' over the phone!"

"Look here!" he says, kinda peeved. "Do you want me to come up there to-night or don't you?"

"Don't you!" I says.

"They's plenty of places where they would be glad to have me to dinner," he snarls. "Places that is just as good as yours!"

"How do *you* know how good they are?" I says. "You ain't never tried no dinners nowheres else but up here."

"They ain't no man can keep me from seein' my cousin!" he says. "Tell Alice I'll be right up!"

I hung up the phone.

"Well," I says to the wife, "I got bad news for you."

"Who was it?" she asks, droppin' the knittin' layout on the floor.

"That trick relative of yours," I tells her. "He's comin' up here for dinner again, so I guess I'll go down to the corner and play a little pinochle."

"You ought to be the weather man," says the wife, "you're such a rotten guesser! You ain't goin' nowheres. You're gonna stay here and help entertain Alex."

"Entertain him?" I says. "What d'ye think I am—a trained seal or somethin'?"

"Don't kid yourself!" she says. "You ain't even makin' the money I could get with a trained seal! You gotta stop this pinochle thing—you don't see Alex wastin' his time playin' pinochle with a lotta loafers!"

"You bet you don't!" I comes back. "You'll never see Alex playin' no game where they's a chance of the other guy winnin'! He wouldn't bet zero was cold! And don't be callin' my friends loafers—every one of them guys is successful business men!"

"That mob you hid out in here one night looked like a lotta plumbers to me!" she says. "Any man who sits up half the night playin' cards is a loafer!"

"One of them loafers I while away my time with lives in the next flat," I says, "and the dumbwaiter door is wide open."

"I don't care," says the wife, flushin' all up. "Let him hear me!"

"I ain't stoppin' him," I says. "But you don't want it to get rumored all over New York that you and me is quarrelin', do you?"

The wife's answer is nothin'. She walks over to the window and looks out on Manhattan, doin' a soft shoe dance with one toe on the floor. If bein' good lookin' was water, she'd be Niagara Falls. You've seen her picture many a time on a can of massage cream—which she never touched in her life! The label claims it was this stuff that put her over, but she don't know whether rouge is for red cheeks or measles. They ain't a day goes by without some movie company pesterin' her to sign up, and she can write her own ticket when it comes to salary. Well, I'm in dutch again, but I don't care! This here knockout is wed to me, and they ain't *nothin'* can give me the blues!

"Listen!" I says. "Honey, we only been wed ten years—and here we are scrappin' *already*!"

She turns on the weeps and I'm across the floor like a startled rabbit. We come to terms in about five minutes, and as far as a disinterested stranger could of seen, everything is O.K. again.

"Well," I says, finally, "you ain't mad at me no more, heh, honey?"

She wags her head, no.

"We got *that* all settled, heh?" I says.

Her head is on my shoulder and why shouldn't it be, and she says yes.

They is a pause. To bust it up, I coughs.

"If that pest Alex wasn't comin' here to-night," I says, "we might go to the theatre."

"The *movies* hurts my eyes!" she answers, givin' me a sarcastical smile.

"D'ye mean to give the neighbors the idea I have never staked you to nothin' but the movies?" I hollers, gettin' sore, naturally enough.

"Don't be callin' my cousin no pest!" she says and—well, we're off again!

In less than five minutes, some new-comers which has a flat across the hall, knocks on the dumbwaiter bell furiously. I answered.

"Why don't you people let go?" inquires a harsh voice. "We can't stand that tourney in there no longer!"

"They ain't no way of puttin' a man in jail for movin'," I says.

"The idea of a man hollerin' at his wife like that!" comes a female voice in back of this guy.

80

"Shut up—I'm doin' this!" exclaims her lovin' spouse,—and then they had a mêlée of their own!

In the middle of this our doorbell rings and in comes Alex.

"They should of named this apartment house the Verdun," he says. "They seems to be a battle goin' on here every time I come up! I could hear every word you people was sayin' as plain as day, away out in the hall!"

"What did you come in for then?" I asks him. "Especially as you could hear this was the rush hour!"

He ignores me and kisses the wife—a thing he knows gets me wild.

"Now, boys!" butts in the wife, splittin' her world famous grin fifty-fifty, "let's stop quarrelin'. They ain't a reason on earth why we can't be friends, even if we are relatives."

"When are you gonna have dinner?" asks Alex.

"This here's eatless night with us," I says. "Not to give you a short answer."

"Don't pay no attention to him, Alex," says the wife. "You know you can eat here whenever you want."

"Sure!" I says. "Don't mind me. All I gotta do is pay for this stuff—that's all!"

The wife gimme a bitter glance.

"That's right," she says. "Tell the world that I have wed a tightwad!"

"What d'ye mean?" I hollers. "I'm as loose as ashes with my money and they ain't nobody knows it better than you. I don't even moan over the monthly phone bill, which from the last one you musta been callin' up friends in Australia!"

"Here!" butts in Alex. "This thing's gotta stop! Come on, kiss and make up. The first thing you know the Red Cross will be openin' a branch here. If I didn't know how much you people loved each other, I'd get the idea that you was really angry."

"Of course we love each other!" I says. "We only pull this now and then so's we won't get sickenin' to the neighbors by billin' and cooin' *all* the time! Ain't I right, honey?"

"Are you sorry?" inquires the wife.

"Sorry?" I says. "Why, I'd go out and buy a tube of carbolic acid if it wasn't so high!"

With that they was peace.

We're just sittin' down to a well-earned meal, when the bell rings again. Actin' as maid is one of the best things I do around my five rooms, if you count the bath, so I answered it. They was a man and a woman standin' there and my heart run up to play with my tonsils when I seen them. I figured they was a couple more guests for dinner and you knew what they're askin' for steak these days.

"I'm sorry to bother you," says the dame, "but we are the people who live in the flat right under yours."

"If you think we're too noisy, moan to the landlord!" I says, "I gotta right to stage an argument in my flat whenever I so choose!"

She giggles. The guy that was with her don't make a sound.

"Why, I'm sure we never heard any noise from above," she says. "I think you and your wife are no doubt the quietest folks in the whole house."

Oh, boy!!!

"How long have you been deaf?" I says.

"You're just like your wife claims," she grins. "Full of life and fun! But I'm keepin' you from your food, ain't I? I wanted to know if you'd let Mister Simmons climb down your fire escape."

"Feed him some veronal," I says, "and he'll no doubt be O.K. in the mornin'. The first day is always tough!"

"Why, what do you mean?" she says. "I merely asked if my husband could climb down your fire escape."

I seen I had wild pitched the first time, so I tried my luck again.

"Is your joint on fire?" I says.

"Oh, no!" she tells me. "But we are locked out. My husband invented a new kind of lock—he's always inventing something that will do everything but work. He put this lock on our door and now he can't open it himself! Isn't that killing?"

"A riot!" I admits. "Come right in."

The wife is gettin' nervous at me bein' out there so long, and when she heard a female voice laughin', of course that didn't help matters none. She meets this dame half way in the hall and the minute they seen each other they fall together in fond embrace. I found out later they'd known each other as long as a week and the last time they met was an hour before.

Well, we get introduced all around and then this bird which invented a lock that nobody on earth could open, includin' himself, goes out on the fire escape followed by his charmin' wife. They entered their flat by the novel method of usin' the kitchen window. This guy didn't open his mouth from the time he come in till he went out, and when spoke to, he blushed all over and acted like he wished to Heaven he could hide under the sofa. His wife, though, had nothin' against conversation as a sport. She was talkin' when she come in and she went out the same way. I never seen nobody in my life who could talk as fast and frequent as this dame and if her husband had hung that trick lock on her tongue he would of made himself solid with me!

"That's that lovely Mrs. Simmons," says the wife, when they had went. "It's too bad her husband ain't a live one."

"Gettin' married has buried many a good man!" I says.

"It didn't change *you* none," she says. "You was a dead one when I got you!"

"Here!" butts in Alex. "Don't you people get started again! I wanna finish my supper in peace. What's wrong with Mister Simmons?"

"He ain't got no pep," says the wife. "They's many a more ambitious man than he is with a tomb around him! He's been keepin' books for twenty dollars a week since the discovery of arithmetic, and he ain't got a raise since they blowed up the *Maine*. He's afraid to ask for more money for fear the boss will find out he's on the pay roll and fire him. They's one ounce more brains in a billiard ball than they is in his head. He—"

"Wait!" interrupts Alex. "This here sounds interestin' to me. In the first place, they ain't a doubt in my mind but what you got that feller figured all wrong! Like all the rest of you simple minded and innocent New Yorkers, you get brains and *imagination* mixed. They is a big difference! *Brains* is what puts a man over, and *imagination* is what keeps him back. The ideal combination is all brains and no imagination! The feller with brains sets his mind on what he wants, forgets everything else, goes to it and gets it. He don't for a minute consider what might happen if he fails, or that the thing he proposes has never been done before, or that maybe his scheme ain't really as good as he first thought it was. Why don't he think of them things? Because he ain't got no imagination! The imaginative feller is beat from the start. He keeps thinkin' from every possible angle, what might happen to him if he *fails* and, by the time he gets that all figured out, his idea is cold and his enthusiasm for it has drowned in the sea of possibilities his roamin' mind has created! The feller which said, 'look before you leap!' might of been clever, but I bet he thought a five-dollar bill was as big as they made 'em till he went to his grave! If I'd had imagination, I'd never of come to New York and made good. I'd of been afraid the town was too big for me. Now this feller Simmons, I'll betcha, is simply sufferin' from a case of too much imagination. He must have *somethin'* in his head or he couldn't even keep books. It takes brains to balance accounts, the same as it takes money to pay 'em. Am I right?"

"What d'ye say, if we go to the movies?" I says.

Alex gets up in disgust.

"Is that all the interest I'm gettin' here?" he asks.

"This ain't no bank!" I tells him.

"Be still!" says the wife. "I heard every word you said, Alex dear. I think you're horribly interestin'. But I still claim Simmons is a fat-head whose butcher bill gives him trouble every month! He never takes that poor wife of his nowheres, but a walk past the Fifth Avenue Library, and she don't know if they have dancin' or swimmin' in cabarets. He's always drawin' things on pieces of paper, and he sits up half the night inventin' what-nots that would be all right, if they wasn't useless."

"Yes," says Alex, "and some day he'll hit on somethin' that'll prob'ly make him famous!"

"I wanna see Beryldine Nearer in 'The Vaccinated Vampire'," I says, reachin' for my hat. "I seen her last week in 'Almost A Fiend' and she was a knockout!"

"Shut up!" says the wife. "What was you sayin', again, Alex?"

"I says it's the dreamer which has made the world what it is to-day," he goes on, strikin' a pose. "He *thinks* of somethin' and the practical feller comes along and makes money out of it. Take—"

"They ain't no man can keep me from the movies!" I butts in. "I ain't gonna be late and only see half of this picture. I done that too often! You and Alice can fight it out amongst yourselves if —"

"All right!" says the wife. "Come on, we'll all go. I admit freely I'm crazy to see Beryldine Nearer again, myself. I seen a gown on her in the last picture which I think I can duplicate in time for Mrs. Martin's card party. We'll ask Mr. and Mrs. Simmons to go with us too. The poor dear, it'll be a treat for her."

"It'll be a treat for her husband, too!" I says. "I ain't gonna take the whole neighborhood to the movies. You must think I'm the Liberty Loan, don't you?"

The wife comes over and kisses me.

"Now, dear," she says. "Don't be so close across the chest. Won't you take 'em for me?"

Well, when all Broadway used to roll over and play dead when she pulled that smile, what chance have *I* got?

"I'd take carbolic for you!" I answers, givin' her a squeeze. "Go ahead, honey, invite the first two pagefuls outa the phone book if you want and I'll take 'em all!"

"There you go," she says. "No wonder we're not wealthy! If it wasn't for me holdin' you down, we wouldn't have a nickel. I'll call down and tell Mrs. Simmons to get ready — they may have an engagement themselves!"

"I doubt if I'm lucky enough for that to happen!" I says.

Well, I missed out again. They come up all right, and Mrs. Simmons is tickled to death. When set for the street, she was a pretty good looker herself, but Simmons ain't even got a hat with him.

"Mister Simmons prefers to stay at home," says his wife, causin' my heart to leap with joy. "He has some important work to do, haven't you, dear?"

Simmons flushes all up.

"Why—eh—yes—quite so—much obliged—excuse me," he stutters, backin' away like he thought I'd wallop him for not goin'.

Alex is lookin' at him strangely.

"Pardon me," he says. "We just been talkin' over some of the wonderful ideas you been workin' on. I have a inventive twist in my brains myself and that lock you put together interests me very much. Could I see it?"

Simmons brightens up in a flash and commences to grin.

"I'd be very glad indeed to show it to you," he says. "Very glad! Its a—"

Alex goes over and puts his arm on his shoulder.

"You folks run along to the movies," he tells us. "Mr. Simmons and me is got a little conference on—eh, Simmons?" He prods him in the ribs and giggles.

Simmons wags his head. A guy with two glass eyes could see he was tickled silly.

I dragged the rest of 'em out.

Well, we come in from the movie around eleven o'clock and stopped in the Simmons flat. They had dragged me into a delicatessen parlor on the way back and put the bee on me for a cold lunch. We was to eat it in Mrs. Simmons's flat. All she furnished was the idea. Alex and Simmons is sittin' in the dinin' room and they're so interested in each other they don't even look up when we come in. The table is full of drawin's and blue prints and scraps of paper all covered over with figures. Simmons is pointin' out somethin' to Alex on a piece of paper, and I'll lay the world four to one Alex ain't got the slightest idea what the other guy's talkin' about, but he's listenin' like he's hearin' the secret of makin' gold outa mud.

"I'll bet you have gone to work and bored Mister Hanley half to death!" says his wife. "How often have I told you that strangers is not interested in them fool ideas of yours?"

"Not at all!" says Alex. "I fail to recall when I spent such a enjoyable night. Mister Simmons is a genius, if they ever was one, and I predict a great future for his automatic cocktail shaker. Then, if he gets his keyless lock workin' right, why—"

"Let's eat in the kitchen, it's cosier," interrupts Mrs. Simmons. "Do you folks mind?"

They was no bloodshed over it, and we all went in. Simmons claims he would like to change his collar, and invites me back to look over the flat, a treat the wife has already had. Once we get in his boudoir, he finds they is everything in the world in it with the exception of a clean collar, and he calls Mrs. Simmons to the rescue.

"Here!" she says, handin' him the laundry. "Hurry up, so's we can eat. He's always losin' somethin'!" she remarks.

I got a comical answer on the tip of my tongue, when Simmons drops his collar button on the floor, and, the same as all the other collar buttons in the world, they picked out the furtherest corners of the room to roll into. The poor boob gets as red as a four-alarm fire and goes crawlin' around the room tryin' to run them collar buttons down.

"It's too bad them buttons wasn't made of rubber," I says, thinkin' to pass the thing off. "They would of bounced right back in your hand, hey?"

He straightens up like he had stepped on a egg and runs his hands through his hair.

"A rubber collar button!" he mutters. "A rubber collar button! No—no—not *rubber*, but—"

"My Gawd!" cuts in Mrs. Simmons. "Will he *ever* stop it? Sit down and eat, folks, he's ravin' again! Here, Edgar, try some of this cold ham. It set our friends back a dollar and it ought to be good!"

"I'm—I'm sorry!" pipes Edgar, movin' away with that little, nervous step of his. "I couldn't eat a thing. I got a headache, I guess—I—excuse me, but I'll see you all again."

With that he blows.

"Ain't he the limit?" inquires Mrs. Simmons, grabbin' the choicest bits of that ham and goin' south with it.

"Mine's worse!" remarks the wife. "What would them men ever do without us?"

"Save money!" I says. "Slip me some of that cold chicken, will you?—I got a stomach, too!"

Well, we didn't see Edgar Simmons no more that night. In fact it was all of two weeks before he appeared again, and then it was by way of the phone. He asked me if I would tell my Cousin Alex to come down at once, he had somethin' very important to tell him. I waited till supper had come and gone that night, and then I got hold of Alex. The wife and Mrs. Simmons went to the theatre together and I arranged the conference for my flat. The minute Alex arrived I phoned Simmons and he come right up. He's all excited over somethin' and he's got a parcel under his arm.

"I have followed your advice," he tells Alex, "and at last I've invented something practical. There's millions in it!"

"What?" I says. "The mint?"

Alex kicks me in the shins under the table so hard that I moaned aloud.

"What is it?" he asks.

Simmons unwraps the parcel and pulls out a piece of cloth. It's the neckband of a shirt and the same as the ordinary neckband in every way—except it's got collar buttons *built right into it*!

"What's the idea?" I asks.

"Heavens, man, can't you grasp it?" says Simmons, slammin' the table with his fist. "Here we have the only collar button in the world *that can't be lost*! You never have to look for it, because it's always attached to the shirt. You can't lose the button unless you lose the shirt! It's made right with it! It—"

"Wait!" butts in Alex, leapin' to his feet. "Simmons—you have got somethin'! Is it patented?"

"Yes," says Simmons.

"Have you felt out the shirt people on it?" asks Alex next.

"That's what I wanted to see *you* about," says Simmons. "I can't get them to look at it! I get shifted from one subordinate to another and they seem to think I'm some sort of a crank. If I could only get it before Philip Calder, the president of the Brown-Calder Shirt Company, I'd be made!"

"Hmm!" grunts Alex. "Well, what d'ye want *me* to do?"

Simmons coughs and fidgets with the button.

"It struck me when you was talkin' to me the other night," he says, "that if there was one man in New York who could see Calder and make him realize the merits of my invention, you were that man! Will you try it?"

"I'll *do* it!" answers Alex. "Gimme the model and you'll hear from me in a few days. Do you wish to sell the neckbands themselves, or just the patent on your idea?"

"I don't care who makes the neckbands," says Simmons, "as long as I get paid for my invention! Of course, I don't expect you to help me for nothing, either."

"Ha! ha!" I butts in. "That bird wouldn't tell you the time for nothing You'll be lucky if you ever even see that invention any more!"

"Don't mind my cousin," Alex tells him. "Outside of a tendency to the measles, he's the worst thing we got in our family! We'll take up the financial end of this later."

Bright and early the next mornin', or eleven o'clock to be exact, Alex invites me to go with him so's I can watch how he would go about seein' the president of the Brown-Calder Company and sellin' him the Simmons patent collar button. As they is always a chance that Alex will fall down, I went along. We had no trouble at all landin' outside the president's office, but once we got there it was different.

"Is Mister Calder in?" says Alex to a blond stenographer, which looks like them movie queens would like to.

She puts four stray hairs back of her left ear and arises.

"Have you got an appointment?" she inquires.

"No," grins Alex, "my nose got that way from bein' hit with a baseball."

She had lovely teeth and showed 'em to us.

"Cards?" she says next, lookin' from one of us to the other.

91

"I'll play these!" says Alex. "Listen! I wanna go in Mister Calder's office without bein' announced. I ain't seen him for years and he'll be tickled silly when we meet. I wanna sneak in and just be there the first time he looks around. I'm a surprise—see?"

She looks kinda doubtful.

"W-e-ll, I don't know," she says. "I've only been here since yesterday, but my orders is to let nobody past this gate without first findin' out their business and so forth. Still and all, I don't wanna be harsh with none of the boss's old college chums or nothin' like that. If you can guarantee I won't lose my job, I'll let you get away with it."

"If you lose your job," says Alex, openin' the gate and pullin' me in after him, "I'll hire you for five dollars more than you're gettin' here. All right?"

"I only trust you're man enough to keep your word," she says. "The boss's office is the first one to the left."

"Thanks," says Alex. "Them eyes of yours is alone worth the trip!"

This guy Calder's door is open and he's sittin' at a big desk writin' away on somethin' like everything depended on speed. He's a great, big fat bird, with one of them trick Chaplin mustaches and he's smokin' a cigar as big as he is. His head is playin' it's hairless day. All in all, he looked like big business, and my knees is knockin' together till I'm afraid he'll hear 'em and turn around. Alex gumshoes up to the desk and without sayin' a word, he lays the neckband right down beside Calder, who immediately swings around with a snort.

"What's all this—how did you get in here?" he bellers.

"We took the subway down from Ninety-sixth Street," says Alex. "That thing you got in your hand is the neckband of a shirt."

"Well?" growls Calder, tappin' the desk with a lead pencil.

"It contains two collar buttons—one front and one back," says Alex. "As you may have noticed, they are built right into the cloth and are meant to come *attached to the shirt*. This does away forever with the necessity of buying a collar button. It cannot be broken, lost or mislaid. Any shirt manufacturer making shirts with this neckband attached will naturally have the bulge on his rivals. I can turn out the neckband for practically nothing. I hold the patent."

Calder sneers.

"Ha!" he says. "There's a million cranks come in my office every day. I suppose you want to sell me this, eh?"

"No, sir!" says Alex, with a pleasant grin.

I liked to fell through the floor at that!

"*No*, sir?" repeats Calder, droppin' the pencil.

"No, sir!" answers Alex.

"Well, what the—what *do* you want then?" roars Calder. "Come now, speak up. I'll give you five minutes, that's all!"

"That's three minutes more than I got to spare!" chirps Alex, pullin' over a chair. "I don't want you to *buy* this neckband, Mister Calder. What I want is this—I know that *you* are the greatest authority on shirts and everything connected with the business, in the United States if not in the world! I think I have a big thing here, a thing that will revolutionize one end of that business. I say I *think* so, because I don't know. Now—the concern I represent wants your opinion of it. We're willing to pay to have you, the world's greatest authority, go on record as to the merits of this invention. If you say it's no good, I'll throw it away and forget about it; if you say it's good, I'll have no trouble placing it anywhere in the world!"

Well, say! That old guy brightens all up when Alex calls him the champion shirtmaker of the world, and pickin' up the band, he turns it over in his hands a few times. You could see that the old salve Alex handed him had gone big!

"Hmph!" he says, finally. "How much would these things cost me?"

"Roughly speakin', about three cents each," says Alex.

"How long will they stand up under laundering?" is the next question Calder fires at him.

"They're the only thing that won't come out in the wash!" answers Alex, without battin' an eye.

The old guy smiles and presses a button. In comes a clerk.

"Send in Mister Lacy, no matter what he's doing, at once!" barks Calder. He turns to Alex as the clerk flees from the room. "Have you been anywhere else with this?" he asks.

Alex looks pained.

"Why, Mister Calder!" he says, "certainly not! Before I went any further I wanted the opinion of the greatest—"

This Lacy guy comes in.

"Mister Lacy is superintendent of our manufacturing department," says Calder. "I'm going to talk with him for three minutes about the effect of the war on the onion crop in Beloochistan. I'll send for you at the expiration of that time. Ah—you can leave the—ah—neckband here!"

"Pardon me!" says Alex, "I have got to be up at the office of the Evers-Raine Shirt Company at three and I can just about make it."

"What the devil are you going to another shirt company for?" roars Calder.

"I have an old friend in the—ah—manufacturing department," says Alex, lookin' straight at him, "who I'm very anxious to see."

Well, they stare at each other for a minute without sayin' a word. They're both playin' poker, and it's Calder who lays his down first!

"Look here!" he grunts. "I'm going to take an option on this infernal thing for a week. How much is that worth to you?"

"Ten thousand dollars," answers Alex, pleasantly.

"I'll pay seven and give you a check right now!" says Calder, slammin' the desk with his fist. "Here, Lacy!" he says to the other guy. "This is what we'll put on our shirts hereafter, unless I'm very much mistaken! What do you think of it?"

Lacy picks up the neckband and looks at it.

"And to think," he mutters in an awed voice. "And to think nobody ever thought of this before!"

"Hmm!" says Calder, takin' the band back. "That's all settled then! Young man," he says to Alex, "the cashier will give you a check. Come back at the end of the week and I'll either give you back your neckband, or a contract for five hundred thousand of them a year for twenty years!"

"Thanks!" says Alex. "Will you have that check certified?"

Well, Simmons like to went insane with joy when we sprung the news on him and Alex insists on him takin' that seven thousand dollar check whole. He didn't ask for a nickel, which had me puzzled. Mrs. Simmons goes out shoppin' for furs, diamonds and automobiles, and the wife asks me why I don't invent somethin', but outside of that they was nothin' more doin' till the end of the week.

95

Then, Alex comes up and breaks the news to Simmons that the Brown-Calder Shirt Company will take all the neckbands that Simmons can supply, as long as people wear shirts.

"We have got to deliver 50,000 in a month," says Alex, "at the rate of two and a half cents apiece. Can you do it?"

Simmons falls back on the sofa in a dead faint!

Well, they was great excitement and the wife finally brings him to life with smellin' salts.

"It was prob'ly the sudden mention of so much money, eh?" I says.

"I'm ruined!" hollers Simmons, leapin' up and dancin' around. "Why, it took me two weeks to make that one miserable model I gave you!" he yells at Alex. "I couldn't make fifty thousand of them things in a lifetime!"

Alexis eyes glitters.

"Here!" he says, slappin' Simmons on the back. "Pull yourself together, man! You've got to think of somethin'. How did you make that one?"

"By hand!" wails Simmons.

"Well, they must be some way of makin' a machine that can turn out so many thousand an hour!" says Alex, walkin' back and forth. "Why—"

"I don't care who makes 'em!" says Simmons. "All I want is to get paid for my idea. I—"

"Listen to me!" interrupts Alex, shakin' him. "Can't you invent some kind of a machine for turnin' them neckbands out?"

"Oh, I had a little something figured out the other night," says Simmons, "but what's the use of me botherin' with that? Why, a machine of that kind would cost at least twenty thousand dollars to make! Where can I get that much money?"

"Look here!" Alex tells him. "You got seven and I'll loan you the balance. You get busy on that machine right away—there's no time to lose!" He grabs his hat. "Come with me and I'll get you the money and then we'll go to my lawyer and draw up a—that is, I'll take your receipt."

That's the last I seen of either of them for a month. At the end of that time, the wife tells me one day that Mr. and Mrs. Simmons is givin' a big dinner that night and that Alex will be there. They'll never notice us no more, if we don't come. Besides, they're goin' for a trip around the country in a few days and this here's a farewell party.

Well, it's a soup and fish affair, and naturally it takes the wife half the night to get dressed up for it. Fin'ly, however, she's dressed to thrill and we blowed in. The minute we did, Simmons pulls me over in a corner where Alex is sittin', smilin' like his name was George Q. Goodhumor.

"Well, sir!" says Simmons, no longer shy and retirin', "I just about cleaned up. My machine is turnin' out three thousand bands an hour, and I get a cent for each and every one!"

"You fin'ly doped out a machine then, heh?" I says.

"Oh, yes!" he tells me. "But unfortunately I don't control it. I have to pay the owner for each band turned out, although it's my invention. But I'm satisfied! I got a bonus of twenty-five thousand dollars from the Brown-Calder people for selling them the exclusive rights to use the neckband, and then we have the foreign rights to—"

"Wait!" I cuts in, turnin' to Alex. All this big money talk was makin' me dizzy. "Where do *you* get off?" I asks him.

"Well, I put the neckband over, didn't I?" he says.

"Yes," I admits, "but Simmons invented it and he gets the royalty. How much cash did he give you?"

"Nothing!" grins Alex.

I looked at Simmons.

"Perfectly correct!" he says, outgrinnin' Alex.

"You—did all that for *nothin'* I hollers, not believin' my ears.

"Well, hardly that," says Alex, lightin' a half-dollar cigar. "You see I loaned Mister Simmons thirteen thousand dollars, if you remember, so that he could make his machine."

"Yeh, yeh!" I says, gettin' impatient. "And—"

"Well, as it stands now," says Alex, "every time the machine turns out a neckband, he gets a cent out of the two and a half cents profit."

"Sure—he told me that!" I says. "But where do *you* get off?"

Alex grins some more.

"I own the machine!" he says. "Have a cigar, cousin?"

CHAPTER V

YOU CAN DO IT!

A guy once said, "Be sure you're right, then go ahead!" and like the bird which invented the sayin', "What are you gonna have?" he became famous on that one line. They's millions of people have repeated both of them remarks since. As far as the last one is concerned, it's about died out now and cracked ice has started gettin' acquainted with lemonade and the like instead of its old haunts, Scotch, Rye and Gin, which has pulled a Rip Van Winkle. I never told no man I was a fortune teller, but if I was a bartender right now, believe me, I'd spend my nights off studyin' the art of makin' chocolate nut sundaes and pineapple ice cream sodas, because the time has come with alarmin' suddenness when alcohol will be used only for rubbin' baby's head when he falls off of the table and the like.

However, that ain't neither here or there, as the guy says which mislaid his watch, so let's get back to the bird which said, "Be sure you're right, then go ahead!" That may be a good line, but it's poor dope for the young. I'll tell the world fair that no winner ever got paid off by stickin' strictly to that. If Columbus had waited till somebody sent him a souvenir postal from the Bronx, so's he'd be sure they really was some choice real estate over here, he never would of discovered America. Napoleon would never of got further than bein' a buck private in the army if he'd of played safe instead of goin' ahead on the "I Should Worry!" plan. I could name a million more guys which got over along the same lines only I hate to walk to the library. But pick up any newspaper and the front page will give you the answer. The guys that go over the top in this well known universe are the boys which goes ahead *first* and figures what chances they got afterwards. They let the results they get tell whether they're *right* or not. I don't mean a guy should bust the traffic laws of any of the prominent virtues in order to be a success, they ain't a game on earth that can't be played on the level and won clean, but instead of askin' yourself, "Can I do it?" say, "This will be *soft* for me!" and you're a odds on favorite to win!

Me and the wife is sittin' down to breakfast one mornin', and I have barely had time to find fault with the eggs when they's a ring at the bell.

"See who that is, will you, dear?" says the wife, turnin' a page of the *Mornin' Shrapnel* and shootin' the smile that used to jam the Winter Garden in my direction. "You know how tired I am in the mornings."

"Yeh," I says, very sarcastical. "Eatin' grape fruit is enough to wear down the strongest. Since how long have I became the maid around here?"

"Before we were married," she says, sinkin' the last of the cream in her coffee—a thing she knows full well practically always enrages me. "Before we was wed, you claimed you'd do anything for me."

"A man can kid, can't he?" I says.

"Don't get catty, dear," says the wife, still featurin' that million dollar smile. "Hurry, there goes the bell again. You really should put on your collar and tie before answering the door, too."

"Who d'ye think is payin' us a call—Wilson?" I says. "I ain't supposed to wear a dress suit in to breakfast, am I?"

They is no answer from the trenches across the table, outside of the munchin' of food, and as our door bell is makin' the telephone green with envy from the way it was ringin', I went out and opened the portals to our flat.

In comes Alex the Great, undisputed champion pest of the world.

He throws his hat on the sofa, kisses the wife, pulls a chair up to the table and reaches over for the paper. Every one of them things is sure fire for gettin' my goat!

"No wonder you people never get nowheres!" he remarks. "Sleepin' away half the day. Here it is eleven o'clock and you just havin' breakfast! I was up at six, had a ice cold bath and walked ten miles."

"I wish you had of made it eleven!" I says.

"Why?" he asks me.

"Because," I says, "that would of brung you a even two blocks past our house and I could of had my breakfast in peace."

"How often have I told you that I don't come here to see you?" he snarls. "If it wasn't for Cousin Alice, I'd never come near your flat!"

"You stayed away a month once," I says, "and she managed to keep out of the hospitals."

"Oh, hush!" says the wife. "You boys are always snappin' at each other. A outsider would think you was in business together or something. How is everything, Alex?"

"Fine!" he says, rubbin' his hands together and castin' a hungry eye over the bacon and eggs. "I already had a breakfast fit for a king, but the early mornin' air gimme a fresh appetite. I think I could stand a little of that bacon and—"

"They's only one piece left," I says, spearin' it with my fork. "Try and get it!"

"Will you be still?" says the wife. "We have plenty in the ice box, Alex, if you want some."

"Don't be blowin' about how much food we got in the ice box," I says. "They may be some spies from Hoover's office around."

"That reminds me," says Alex, makin' the best of it by devourin' all the crackers and jam. "I expect to go to Washington this week and offer my services to Mister Hoover."

"What was you thinkin' of doing for Mister Hoover, Alex?" says the wife.

"I got a scheme for—," he begins, when I ceased firin' on the bacon and eggs and arose.

"Listen!" I butts in. "I don't like to walk out in the middle of your act, Alex, but I gotta date. I have just bought a infielder from Jersey City which they tell me is a second Ty Cobb. The last guy which come recommended to me like that acted like hittin' the ball was a felony and he must of figured that droppin' grounders put Cobb over. I have give everything but the franchise for this new bird, and I wanna see right now if he's one of them things or a ball player."

"Don't make no engagements for to-night," says the wife, "because we're goin' to the movies with them lovely Wilkinsons."

"Who's them lovely Wilkinsons?" I says.

"You could spend a year at the bottom of the ocean and never get acquainted with a fish!" says the wife. "The Wilkinsons is the people which just moved in across the hall. Her husband is a salesman for a big wholesale clothing house downtown and if you're nice to him he can prob'ly get you a raincoat or something, for a great deal different price than you'd pay yourself."

"Yeh," I says. "It would no doubt cost me about ten bucks *more*, if I bought it from him! I know them birds. That guy will gimme his card and send me down to the foundry where he works, and they'll sell me somethin' which has graced their shelves for the last ten years, at ten per cent over the retail price. The public will laugh me outa wearin' it and, on top of that, this guy will want the first five rows at the world's series for doin' me the favor! Anyways, I don't need no raincoat, I got two already."

"I never seen nobody like you," says the wife. "I'll bet you think the war was a frame-up! Accordin' to you, nobody or nothin' is on the level, and the whole world and Yonkers is out to give you the work. I have already talked with Mister Wilkinson, which is a nice little innocent fellow and not a brute like you which battles night and day with his wife, and he will have a raincoat up here for you to-morrow."

I threw up my hands!

"How much is it?" I says.

"Practically nothin'," says the wife. "Forty-five dollars."

Oh, boy!

"Listen!" I says, openin' the door. "Unless that bird has give you his age in mistake for the price of the raincoat, you can tell him that if I had forty-five bucks to hurl away like that I wouldn't wear no raincoat. I wouldn't care if it rained or not!"

"It's one of the latest trench models," says the wife. "I got two of them. One for myself."

"You and that lovely little Wilkinson will have to shoot craps for them then!" I hollers. "I wouldn't let him take me for ninety bucks if—"

"They are both paid for long ago," smiles the wife, pinchin' my cheek, and pullin' the smile that used to get her photo in the magazines. "I give him a check last week!"

As unfortunately I am nothin' but human, I beat it before they was violence and bloodshed. I was afraid to trust myself with speech, but I managed to let off a little steam before I left by throwin' three pillows and a Rumanian beer stein at Alex, havin' caught him grinnin' at me like a idiot.

It was about six hours before I got back and my temper had failed to improve with age, havin' had a rough day at the ball park. We played a double-header with the Phillies and lost a even two games. Both the scores sounded more like Rockefeller's income tax than anything else. Iron Man Swain pitched the first game for us and before five innin's had come and went, I found out that the only thing iron about him was his nerve in drawin' wages as a pitcher. Everybody connected with the Philly team but the batboy got a hit and from the way them guys run around the bases it looked more like a six-day race than a ball game!

I sent in Red Mitchel to pitch the second half of the massacre, and all he had was a boil on his arm. As far as his offerin's was concerned, everybody on the Philly club could of been christened Home Run Baker. When he throwed the ball on the clubhouse roof tryin' to get a guy nappin' off first, lettin' in two extry runs instead, I went out to the box and removed him by hand. Ed Raymond finished the game for us, and he's so scared we might win it that he walks the first three men and knocks the fourth guy cold with a inshoot. I didn't even stay to see the finish—I had enough!

One of the features of the day was the work of this so-called "Second Ty Cobb" at short. He come to bat eleven times in the two games and got one hit. That was a left jab from the Philly first baseman which got peeved at bein' called a liar and bounced one off the Second Ty Cobb's ear. At fieldin' he made more errors than the Kaiser and was just as popular with the crowd. I give up five thousand berries and a outfielder for him, and after them two games I couldn't of sold him as a watch charm to the manager of a high school club!

From all of this you may get an idea of the sweet humor I was in when I blowed into the flat that night. My idea was to put on the feed bag, and then go around to the corner and play a little pinochle with the gang. Like the guy which fell off Washington's Monument I was doomed to disappointment, because they was quite a little reception committee awaitin' me. Among them present besides the wife was Alex and them lovely Wilkinsons.

The lovely Wilkinsons consisted of the regular set—husband and wife. They had only been wed about three weeks, new time, and from the way they behaved towards each other, a innocent bystander would think they had only staggered away from the altar a hour before. They sit together on the sofa, three inches closer to each other than the paper is to the wall and both of them must of been palmists judgin' from the way they hung on to each other's hands. The male of the layout is a husky kid which either come direct from one of the college football teams or had just knocked off posin' for the lingerie ads in the subway. The female would of been a knockout, if my wife had been in Denver, but bein' in the same room with her the best Mrs. Wilkinson could do was to finish a good second. They is one thing about the wife, they may be dames which can knit sweaters faster than her, but when it comes to bein' excitin' to gaze upon she leads the league! I don't have to tell the world that, the world keeps tellin' it to me. This here is far from our first season as matrimoniacs, and when I say that it still makes me dizzy to look at her, you may get a idea of how she checks up.

But to get back to them lovely Wilkinsons, they are sittin' there on the sofa keepin' a close eye on each other, and Alex is givin' 'em everything he's got in the line of chatter. They're both payin' the same undivided attention to him that the Board of Aldermen in Afghanistan pays to the primaries in Bird's Nest, Va. Them babies is too busy gazin' on each other and bein' happy, and while that stuff gets silly at times—they is worse things than that.

After we have got the introductions all took care of, the wife rushes me down to Delicatessen Row to grab off some extry food on account of these added starters at our modest evenin' meal. I got a armful of these here liberty links, *née* frankfurters, and some liberty cabbage which before the Kaiser went nutty was knowed as sauerkraut. They ain't no use callin' off all the other little trinkets I got to help make the table look tasty, especially as Mister Hoover is liable to scan this and I don't wanna get myself in wrong, but when I got through shoppin' I didn't have enough change left out of a five-case note to stake myself to a joyride in the subway.

Just as we're goin' to the post in this supper handicap, the bell rings, and in come Eve, which same is no less than the blushin' bride of Alex. They is now so many people in the flat that for all the neighbors know I have opened up a gamblin' dive or one of them cabaret things. Everybody is talkin', with the exception of me, which havin' sit down to eat proceeded to do so with the greatest abandon, as the guy says. Them three girls—the wife, the lovely Mrs. Wilkinson and Eve, was sure some layout to have across the table, I'll tell the world fair! They had the front row of the Follies lookin' like washwomen durin' the rush hour, and all I did was sit there and eat and wonder how in Heaven's name they ever come to fall for a set of guys like me, Alex and the lovely Wilkinson.

Well, the meal come to an end without no violence, and they was only one time when it seemed like boxin' gloves would be needed. Even that wasn't exactly *my* fault. From the general chatter of the lovely Wilkinson, I figured him as a big, fatheaded, good-lookin' bonehead whose greatest trick so far had been marryin' his wife. He got my goat a coupla times hand runnin' by dealin' himself, first, the last piece of bread and, second, the last potato on the table. Either one of them things would of enraged me by themselves, but pullin' 'em together was a open dare to me to commit homicide. I laid for him for a half hour and fin'ly I get a openin'.

"Mister Wilkinson is packed to the ears with ambition," says the wife to me across the table. "He expects to fall into a lot of money very shortly."

"I don't see how they can be no room for him to be packed with nothin' else," I says, "after all the meat and potatoes he put away to-night. And as far as that fallin' into a lot of money is concerned, he must be figurin' on stumblin' at the door of the mint, hey?"

They is a dead silence and the lovely Wilkinson give a nervous snicker and piled up his plate with liberty links and cabbage to hide his confusion. Alex laughs like a hyena and Mrs. Wilkinson looks even prettier when mad than she did when tryin' to be a charmin' guest. The wife gimme a glance that would of killed a guy with a weaker heart and tries to laugh it off.

"You mustn't mind him," she says. "He's always kiddin' that way about everything. Really—I'm—I'm so angry I don't know what to do!"

"I'll tell you what to do," I says. "See if you can get the embargo lifted on that food down at your end of the table and ease a little nourishment up here!"

"He oughta leave the table!" remarks Alex.

"You ain't talkin' to me!" I says. "I'm wonderin' if you guys will leave the table or not. You already have eat everything else!"

"That's right!" says the wife. "Go ahead and advertise the fact that I have married a roughneck!"

"My neck must of got that way from wearin' that sweater you knit me," I says. "Hey, dearie?"

Eve gimme a laugh, but I seen the wife was gettin' ready to bring up the heavy artillery so I laid off.

While the girls is seein' what soap and water will do to a pail of dishes, I released some cigars and us strong men had a even stronger smoke. The lovely Wilkinson seems to have somethin' on his mind and says practically nothin', both when he talked and when he didn't. Alex kids me about my ball team and, finely, the household cares bein' attended to in the kitchen, we all set sail for the movies.

The wife calls me aside, gimme a kiss and says for me to buy the tickets. Of course after she done that I don't have to tell you who pushed the quarters in under the cashier's window. The picture we seen was one of them forty-eight reel thrillers and was called "Lunatic Lily's Lover" or somethin' like that. They was a guy killed in every reel but the first one. They was three killed in that. The picture must of been made by the local branch of the suicide club, assisted by a lot of candidates for the insane asylum. I'll tell the world that the guy which wrote the scenario had at least delirium tremens. The girls thought it was great, but I knew better and put in my time figurin' out on the back of a envelope how many games we had to lose to be in last place by August.

The lovely Wilkinson gets very talkative once inside the theatre. He starts right in on the picture and claims it's a awful thing. Every time a guy goes over a cliff or dives off of a bridge and all the salesladies and bankers sittin' around us gasps out loud, he speaks up and says it's all faked with a trick camera and they ain't none of them really doin' nothin' at all. He claims he's got a friend which used to sell tickets for a movie theatre and he told him all about it. The more stunts the hero of this picture does, the worse the lovely Wilkinson gets, and it ain't long before he has captured the goat of friend Alex, which is champion moving picture fan of the United States and Coney Island. When the lovely Wilkinson claims that nobody in real life could do the tricks this movie hero was pullin' off, Alex butts in.

"How do *you* know them things can't be done?" he says.

"Anybody but an idiot could see that!" says Wilkinson. "The idea of trying to make intelligent people believe that this fellow with his hair brushed back like a rabbit's could sell one of those wealthy millionaires gold mines and the like. Why, he'd be thrown out of the office and—"

"No wonder you ain't a success!" butts in Alex.

The lovely Wilkinson shows a little spirit.

"How do you know I ain't a success?" he says. "I'm making my good twenty-five dollars each and every week."

"Yeh?" sneers Alex. "I once heard tell of a feller which was makin' thirty, but I ain't sure of it because none of the newspapers said a word about it." He turns around and lowers his voice on account of some hisses comin' from fans in the back. "Look here!" he says. "All jokes to one side, they ain't nothin' that this feller done in the picture that can't be done by anybody. A man can do anything he wants to, *anything*, they ain't no limit—if he's got enough sand to fight his way through whatever stands in his way! I don't care what the thing is he wants, a man can get anything if he keeps tryin' and—"

"You hate yourself, don't you?" butts in the lovely Wilkinson, peevishly. "I suppose you think *you* could do anything—"

"I do not," says Alex. "I *know* it! I ain't talkin' about myself though, I'm talkin' about you. You're a young married feller with a sweet, beautiful, and, for all I know, sensible little wife. You people are just startin' out, and I want to see you make good. I think you got the stuff in you somewheres, but not to be rough or nothin' of the sort, I must say you have been a success at concealin' it so far. Twenty-five dollars a week ain't enough wages for nobody—as long as they's somebody makin' twenty-six—understand? And if you get where they pay you twenty-five dollars a *minute* instead of a week, you wanna try and make 'em think you're worth thirty! The mistake you and a lot of young fellers make is quittin' at a given point. They ain't no point to quit! I bet when you was makin' eighteen dollars a week you hustled like blazes to make twenty, but when you got up to twenty-five you prob'ly told yourself that you was makin' as much as most of the boys you knew and more than some, so why wear yourself out and slave for a fatheaded boss, eh? Right in sight of the grandstand you blew up and quit in the stretch. I bet you think right now that you're makin' good because you're holdin' down the job, hey? That ain't makin' good, that's stealin' the boss's money—petty larceny, and deprivin' your future kids of a even chance—a felony! Give the boss everything you got, and he'll pay for it. If he don't, get out and dive in somewheres else! They ain't no place on earth where they ain't a openin' for a live one at any hour of the day or night!"

The lovely Wilkinson says nothin'.

Pretty soon and much to my delight, this here picture comes to a end, and while we're goin' out in the lobby, the lovely Wilkinson calls his wife aside and whispers somethin' in her ear. It ain't over a second later that we're all invited up to the Wilkinson flat for a little bite and the like before retirin'.

The girls starts a hot and no doubt interestin' argument about how many purls make a knit and so forth, and the lovely Wilkinson, after fidgetin' around a bit, calls us into another room. He closes the door very careful.

"I got something very personal and very important I'd like to speak to you about," he says to Alex.

"I'll go out on the fire escape," I says.

"No!" he says. "I want you to stay and hear this too." He turns to Alex again. "I been thinking over what you said in the theatre to-night," he begins, "and I guess you're pretty near right about me. However, I have a big chance now to make good and get out of the twenty-five dollar class, only, as usual, luck is against me."

"They is no such thing as luck," says Alex. "Forget about that luck thing, put the letter 'P' before the word and you got it! That's the first rule in my booklet, 'Success While You Wait.' I must send you one."

"Thanks," says the lovely Wilkinson. "You see, I'm a salesman for a big wholesale clothing house downtown and right at the beginning of the war I went up to Plattsburg to try for a commission in the army. I was rejected on account of a bad eye. While I was up there, I met Colonel Williams, who is now practically in charge of the buying of equipment for the army. I've been trying for months to land the overcoat contract for my house and last week I finally got things lined up. I have got to have one thousand of our storm-proof army coats in Washington by five o'clock to-morrow afternoon. At that time, Colonel Williams will see me at the War Department and I can give him prices on various lots and so forth."

"Why do you have to bring that many coats down?" asks Alex. "Wouldn't a couple be enough for a sample?"

"No," says Wilkinson. "These coats are to be given to men in a cantonment near Washington, where they will get actual wear under varying conditions. If I'm not in Washington with them at five to-morrow, I'll lose my chance because, the following day, men from four rival houses have appointments with the Colonel."

"Well," I butts in, "what's stoppin' you from goin' to Washington?"

"Nothing is stopping *me*," he says, "but I can't get the coats down there with me in time! The two shipments that we have sent by freight have gone astray somewhere and, as government supplies have the right of way over all other shipments, the express companies will not guarantee a delivery at any set time."

"But them coats are government supplies, ain't they?" says Alex.

"Not yet!" says the lovely Wilkinson. "Not until they are accepted. Right now they are nothing but samples of clothing. I've gone into that part thoroughly."

Alex gets up and walks around the room a coupla times, throwin' up a smoke screen from his cigar. Then he stops and looks at his watch.

"It's now almost eleven o'clock," he says. "Where are them coats?"

The lovely Wilkinson looks puzzled.

"Why," he says. "Why—they're in our stock room at 245 Broadway."

"Can we get in there to-night?" asks Alex, reachin' for his hat.

"I have a key," says Wilkinson, "but I'm afraid I don't quite get the idea. I—"

"Look here!" says Alex, very brisk. "I'm goin' to deliver you and one thousand of them overcoats outside the War Department in Washington at five o'clock to-morrow afternoon! What will you get if you land this order?"

The lovely Wilkinson leaps out of his chair.

"Why—I—," he splutters, "I—get fifteen per cent if—but you can't get the coats there, it's impossible! Why—"

"Never let me hear you use that word impossible' again!" snorts Alex. "Speak United States! I spent a half hour to-night tellin' you that a man can do *anything* if he wants to. Now look here, they ain't no time to lose. I'll land you and your coats in Washington to-morrow on time. That will cost your firm around a thousand dollars—the same bein' the price of the means of locomotion. I will take your word of honor that you will pay me twenty per cent of any profits you make on any order you take as a result of my efforts. Is it a bargain? Speak quick!"

"If you are thinking of getting a special train," says Wilkinson, "it can't be—"

"Yes or no!" hollers Alex. "I'll take care of the rest!"

"Yes!" yells the lovely Wilkinson, jumpin' around like some of Alex's pep has entered his system. "If you put this over for me, I'll give you *half* of anything I get!"

"You're gonna put it over yourself!" says Alex. "Now listen to me. You grab a taxi and beat it down to your stock room. Get them overcoats ready and in about a hour I'll call there for you. We're goin' to Washington to-night and don't be over five minutes sayin' good-by to your wife!"

"But—" says Wilkinson, lookin' like Alex had him hypnotized.

"Git!" bawls Alex, and slams a hat on the lovely Wilkinson's head.

Well, within four minutes the lovely Wilkinson has beat it, leavin' behind a astounded and weepin' wife and Alex is on the phone callin' up the Gaflooey Auto Company's service station and in ten minutes more he has arranged to have a truck and a mechanic chug-chuggin' outside the house. Then he turns to me.

"Here is another chance for you to lose some dough," he says. "I'm gonna take Wilkinson and his trick overcoats down to Washington by way of a auto truck. If we leave here at midnight, we got about seventeen hours to make 225 miles, that's an average of around thirteen miles a hour. The Gaflooey one-ton truck can make twenty, if chased. Of course we may hit some bum roads or lose the carburetor and so forth, which might delay us some. What'll you bet I don't put this over?"

I walked over to the window and looked out at New York. They is one of them rains fallin' that generally plays a week stand before passin' on to the next village. I figured that trip in the middle of the night, the rain and the tough goin'.

"Gimme a proposition," I says.

"All right," says Alex. "Me and Eve needs some furniture for the library. I'll bet you fifteen hundred against a thousand that I get Wilkinson in Washington in time to put over his deal."

"I got you," I says. "If he gets there too late to put over anything with the War Department, I win—right?"

"Correct!" says Alex. "And now have Cousin Alice put up some sandwiches and the like for us. I got a lot to do!"

Well, at five minutes to twelve that night they was a Gaflooey truck gasolined its merry way aboard a Forty-second Street ferry. On board it was Alex, the lovely Wilkinson, one thousand storm-proof army overcoats and yours in the faith.

I ain't liable to forget that trip for a long while to come, because I got soaked to the skin—with water—and just missed gettin' pneumonia by one cough. The rain kept gettin' worse and worse and it hadn't a thing on the roads. We went through Trenton, N. J., along around 4 a.m. in a storm that would of made the Flood look like fallin' dew. The mud is up over the hubs of the truck, but it keeps plowin' along at a steady gait with Alex and the mechanic takin' turns at the wheel. I crawled in under some of them one thousand overcoats at Philly and went to sleep, the last I heard bein' the lovely and half-drowned Wilkinson callin' out the time every fifteen minutes and moanin', "We'll never make it!"

Mornin' brung no let up in the rain, but the old Gaflooey truck keeps thunderin' on. Sometimes we done five miles a hour, sometimes twenty and when this big baby was goin' twenty, believe me, it was rough sleddin'! We run into a bridge at Wilmington, Del., and at Baltimore we bumped a Flivver off of the road, but outside of that they was nothin' but rain and mud and the lovely Wilkinson complainin' about the dampness, like he was the only one that was gettin' a endless cold shower.

It was twenty minutes of five when we rolled into the city limits of Washington and I'll tell the world we was a rough lookin' bunch. Alex is grinnin' from ear to ear and slappin' Wilkinson on the back and this guy has perked up a bit, though wishin' out loud that he was home with coffee, bacon and eggs and Mrs. Wilkinson. I am cursin' the day that ever brung Alex into our family circle and wonderin' if death by double pneumonia is painful. The mechanic is fallin' asleep at the wheel, wakin' himself up from time to time with shots out of a flask and of lemon ice-cream sodas or something he had on his hip.

We stopped in front of the War Department and Alex says we better straighten up ourselves and the overcoats before callin' on Colonel Williams. At that, the mechanic falls off the seat and dives into a restaurant and we go back to look at the coats.

"If any of us had any brains," says Alex, jerkin' a coat off the pile, "we would all of worn one of these here things and kept nice and dry—*Sufferin mackerel!*" he winds up all of a sudden.

Me and the lovely Wilkinson swings around and there's Alex holdin' up the coat.

Oh, boy!!!!!

This here storm-proof army coat, which Wilkinson hoped to unload on the U. S. army, just simply fell apart in his hands! He grabbed another and another—and they're all alike. The rain has took all the color outa them, they have shrunk till they is hardly enough cloth to accommodate the buttons and the linin's, which was supposed to be leather, has fell right to shreds from the water. All in all, they was nothin' but a mess of soggy, muddy rags which no self-respectin' junk dealer would of took for a gift!

The lovely Wilkinson's face is a picture. He's as pale as the mornin' cream and I thought for a minute he was gonna bust out cryin'. I couldn't help feelin' sorry for the kid, but when I thought of that wild night ride through the rain and mud to bring this bunch of garbage to Washington, I wanted to laugh out loud! And then I remember Alex bettin' me Wilkinson would take the order, and I haw-hawed myself silly, right there in the street.

"Shut up!" barks Alex, swingin' around on me. "This here is far from a laughin' matter. It's pretty serious business!" He turns to Wilkinson and shakes him by the shoulder. "Young man," he snaps, "is that the kind of stuff you were goin' to put on our boys which fought for you in France?"

Wilkinson is lookin' at the coats like they fascinated him.

"Why—why this is terrible!" he stammers, fin'ly. "They told me— why—Good Heavens, you don't think *I* knew these things were made up like this, do you?"

Alex studies him for a minute.

"No," he says, "I don't! You don't look like you'd do that, anyways. What's the name of your firm?"

"Gerhardt and Schmidt," says Wilkinson. "I know it sounds German, but both members of the firm have been naturalized and —"

"Never mind that," says Alex. "Even if it wasn't no worse than a scheme to clean up on a government contract, I think the Secret Service will be interested in seein' them coats!"

The lovely Wilkinson sits right down on the curb and buries his face in his hands.

"Good night!" he moans. "I'm done for now. I thought this was going to be a big thing for me and —"

Alex slaps him on the back.

"No whinin'," he says. "We're still in Washington—you can't tell what might happen yet."

"You can gimme that fifteen hundred berries right now if you want, Alex," I says, "because I'm gonna grab the next train for Manhattan. This is *one* that beat you and —"

"Ssh!" says the lovely Wilkinson, jumpin' up suddenly. "Here comes Colonel Williams himself!"

We looked around and sure enough there's two army officers walkin' over to the War Department. When they got opposite us, Wilkinson braces himself and steps forward.

"Pardon me, Colonel," he says. "I'm Mister Wilkinson of Gerhardt and Schmidt. I had an appointment with you to-day at five to show you those army coats."

The Colonel looks at him.

"Oh, yes," he says, very pleasant. "Just step inside, Mister Wilkinson. I'll see you in my office. You are very prompt. You must have been caught in the downpour—you're soaking wet."

116

"Yes, sir," says Wilkinson. "I—ah—Colonel, I don't think there's any use of me stepping into your office."

"Eh—why not?" says the Colonel.

Wilkinson turns several of the popular colors.

"I—ah—the fact is," he says, "our coat is not what the United States government wants, Colonel. I didn't know it at the time I solicited the contract—I—I've just found it out. We brought the required number of coats down here by auto truck, not being able to get them here on time by freight or express. The trip was made in yesterday's storm and"—he points to the mess on the truck—"there's the coats!"

The Colonel examines a couple of them soggy rags and he gets very severe. I heard him say somethin' that sounded like "Damn!" a couple of times, and then he turns to Wilkinson.

"This is a matter for the Department of Justice," he says. "You will leave the truck and its load right here, Mister Wilkinson, and I'll personally see that it's taken care of. Your action in coming direct to me with this evidence is commendable. You may telegraph your firm that the United States government is holding this shipment for investigation. I'm sorry for your sake that this happened, as I had all but made up my mind to give you the contract. If you desire to see me further, I'll be in my office until six."

With that he stamps away. The other officer who was with him has been walkin' around the Gaflooey truck all the time and examin' it like it's the first auto he ever seen in his life.

"Pardon me," he says to Wilkinson, "did I understand you to say that you made the trip from New York yesterday in the storm on this truck?"

"Yes, sir," says Wilkinson.

The officer pulls out a notebook.

"What time did you leave New York?" he asks, very businesslike.

Wilkinson tells him. Then the officer asks if we had any trouble, how much gas and oil we used, what was our average speed and a million other things. Alex's eyes begin to dance around, and he winks at me like there's somethin' in the air. Fin'ly the officer walks away, after thankin' the lovely Wilkinson for the information.

"Now!" hollers Alex, grabbin' Wilkinson's arm. "You win!"

"Win?" moans Wilkinson. "I'll be lucky if I don't go to jail!"

"You're crazy!" bellers Alex, gettin' more and more excited. "You had nothin' to do with this thing—you didn't know the coats was no good. Forget about that, the thing is you got a chance right now to put over a bigger thing than them overcoats. You come here to make a sale, didn't you? All right, go to it! That officer is connected with the purchasin' department of the government, and he wasted a lot of time talkin' to you about that truck. Do you realize what a wonderful thing that was to get down here O.K. in that terrible storm yesterday? No—*you* don't, but *he* did! Right now he's got that there truck on his mind. Go after him before he gets inside the buildin' and make your sale!"

"But," says Wilkinson, kinda dazed, "what have I got to sell? The overcoats are—"

"Damn the overcoats!" hollers Alex. "Sell him the truck that brought 'em down—they ain't nothin' wrong with that! If it's good enough for a trip like that, it's good enough for the army, ain't it? Hurry up and make an appointment with him for to-day, and I'll get you the figures on the Gaflooey truck for a hundred or a million—I know 'em by heart!"

"By Heavens, I'll chance it!" says Wilkinson, and runs after the officer.

Comin' up on the train that night I sit in the smoker and write Alex my check for a thousand berries. They was no two ways about it as he showed me, because he had bet he would make Wilkinson put over a sale in Washington. He didn't say *what* he had to sell. The lovely Wilkinson, which has sent about five dollars' worth of night letters to his wife, is sittin' on the other side, delirious with joy and with a order in his pocket for one thousand Gaflooey trucks as per the one we come down in. Alex had wired the Gaflooey people and had Wilkinson appointed a salesman for the Washington territory on his recommendation. Them guys would do anything for Alex, because he put 'em on the map. With telegraphed credentials from New York, the rest was a cinch for even the lovely Wilkinson, because the truck sold itself!

"They is only one thing that beats me," I says to Alex before we turn in on the sleeper. "Why didn't *you* sell the truck and make all the dough yourself?"

"Its a good thing you don't need brains in your game," says Alex, "or you and Alice would starve! I wanted Wilkinson to make the sale all by himself, because it will give him confidence, and then, again, he'll advertise me. I get half of his commission, I grab a bonus from the Gaflooey people for helpin' the sale along and then there's that thousand bucks of yours, which I would of lost if I sold the trucks myself. Also, I have put Mister Wilkinson over, and that's what I started out to do!"

"You win!" I says. "I don't see how you get away with it. It's past me!"

"Huh!" says Alex. "They ain't no trick to it at all—why say, even *you* could of done it!"

CHAPTER VI

THE LITTLE THINGS DON'T COUNT

They's many a guy clutterin' up a pay roll for about thirty bucks a week, which has got more brains than his boss has income tax. When he went to school they wasn't a day that some other kid didn't wanna murder him because he got 100 in arithmetic and the like. He passed on to high school and even invaded college, where he dumfounded all in hearing with his knowledge of—everything! When he was fin'ly turned loose on a helpless world, he was so far ahead of his class that they held special services for him and had the regular one the next day.

Now the dope oughta be that this marvel of intelligence should be down in Wall Street now, tellin' J. P. Morgan and etc. that the next time they come in late for work he'd fire 'em. Well, about once in ten thousand times this is true. Usually, however, this guy is the bird that takes your card at the office door and says, "Sit down, Mr. Morgan's fifth assistant secretary will see you in a moment." And then the head bookkeeper rings a bell and this guy says, "Yes, sir," and jumps!

They is a reason for this, the same as for everything else outside of the Kaiser. The swell-dressed assassin with the ladies, which writes such beautiful figures and knows offhand how much is thirty-three times eighty, is fast joinin' the list of non-essential industrials. They got a machine now which can count better than him, and don't try to make no date with the stenographer, either! He thinks his boss is a boob, because said boss is a little bit in doubt as to what day of the week Napoleon joined the army, and he wonders how in heaven's name a guy as stupid as that ever got as far as he did. The answer to that one is easy. While *he* was memorizin' the fact that A plus C equals X, his *boss* was figurin' how to hire a brainy guy like him to count his dough!

The wife and I are about to set sail for the movies one night, when our French maid from the Bronx admits a interruption by the name of Alex.

"Well," he says, kidnappin' my goat by treatin' himself to one of my pet cigars, "I have run across another feller which I am on the verge of makin' a success. I've studied his case carefully and all he needs is to be set on the right track to bust all speed records."

"Where did you meet this second-story man?" I says.

"He ain't no burglar," says Alex; "he's some kind of a bookkeeper, and he's got one of the sweetest little girls in love with him you ever seen!"

"I thought you was married," I says.

"Now," says Alex, snubbin' me as usual, "I want to bring him up here to dinner to-morrow night and have you meet him as he is at present. In a short time later I'll bring him back again, and if he hasn't made himself a success, I'll buy you all the best dinner you ever eat!"

"Listen!" I says. "As Hoover says, 'Food will win the war—don't eat it!' Don't be invitin' no more guys up here to dinner. It's tough enough to have to feed *you* three or four times a week, without you ringin' in these guys which acts like I win them steaks and chops in a raffle. Now I'm goin' to the movies. They's a five-reeler down at the corner called 'She Give Her Soul!' and they ain't no man gonna keep me from seein' that to-night."

"Come along with us, Alex," chimes in the wife. "A couple of my girl friends which used to be in the Winter Garden with me is in this picture and I'm crazy to see them!"

"Hmph!" snorts Alex. "Anybody is crazy which pays money to look at them fool movin' pictures. If I had my way, they'd all be stopped and—"

"Lillian Dish is in this one," butts in the wife. "Have you seen her lately?"

"No!" says Alex, jumpin' up. "By mackerel, I haven't! Hurry up, we'll be late—you people is never in time for anything! Lillian Dish, hey? Say! Did you see her in 'What's a Wife?' She was great! Why I—"

I dragged the both of them out.

Promptly at seven the next night Alex comes up with his new-found friend. I let forth a groan and told the maid to lay a couple more plates, but to slice everything as thin as possible without cuttin' her hands. The stranger was a tall, slim bird which wouldn't have been bad-looking if he hadn't been so serious. He acted like it was a felony to smile, and got my name wrong the first four times he repeated it.

Well, after the sound of clashin' knives and forks had died away, the wife dolls all up and goes over to visit the hero which wed Alex; and us strong men repairs to the parlor, where the cigars clink merrily and the like.

The stranger's name turned out to be S. Jared Rushton, and after a while I figured the "S" stood for "Silly." This guy knowed more about figures than the stage manager at the Follies. He was a hound for numbers, dates and etc. He had a better memory than a loan shark, and a encyclopedia would look stupid alongside of him. No matter what the subject was, this guy knowed more about it than the bird which wrote it and would butt in with the figures to prove it. Fin'ly, when I struck a match and he tells me they is 9,765,543 of them used in New York every fiscal year, I went out into the kitchen for air!

At first it was kinda interestin' and entertainin' to get the inside dope on *everything* at practically no cost, but they is such a thing as bein' *too* clever; and when it become impossible to speak of anything on earth from bankin' to beer, without this bird buttin' in with all the figures on it, I got enough! I tried to yawn him into goin' home, and he notices I got two bum teeth. That furnished him with a scenario for tellin' me that every year 490,517 people is treated by dentists in New York alone, and I says I can't help it and he mustn't of got a wink or sleep the night he counted 'em.

I struck a match and he tells me they is 9,765,543 of them used in New York every fiscal year.

"Oh," he says, "it's very simple. I carry all those figures in my head."

"Why not?" I says. "They's plenty of room there!"

He looked kinda peeved; but before he could come back at me, Alex takes things in hand.

"Jared," he says, "you are certainly a educated citizen. With all them interestin' facts and figures in your head you must be very valuable to the firm you work for, hey?"

Jared throws out what chest he had with him.

"Well," he says, "I saved the Hamilton Construction Company just $6,547.98 last year by cutting down the excessive use of lead pencils and blotters alone!"

"That's fine!" says Alex. "No doubt they give you a handsome bonus for that, hey?"

"Of course," says Jared. "They raised my salary to thirty-five dollars a week. I was only getting thirty-two and a half."

"You saved them six thousand last year and they raised you about a hundred and thirty, eh?" says Alex. "Now, listen! Why couldn't you have made that six thousand for *yourself* just as easy?"

"Why—I—why—" stammers Jared. "I have no chance to make anything but my salary. I'm simply working there, and—"

"And you always will be, if you don't get wise to yourself!" butts in Alex. "Your boss—"

"My boss, eh?" sneers Jared. "Say, he hasn't got the brains of a gnat! He'd be absolutely up in the air if I wasn't at his elbow with data and estimates on everything. He doesn't know anything, and—"

"No, I guess not!" butts in Alex, with a odd grin. "He don't know anything—only how to make money! Say, listen! If this boss of yours is such a boob, what must *you* be? You're *workin'* for him, ain't you? Why should he have any brains, when he can rent yours for thirty-five dollars a week? Now, listen to me, son. You know a little about everything on earth, with the slight exception of yourself! The figures that should interest you more than anything else is these: For every dollar *you* make, your boob boss is makin' a thousand. Ever figure them statistics along with the other stuff?"

Jared registers embarrassment. "Look here!" he says. "I really don't see the reason of all this. I consider myself quite successful. I may not be making a million a week, but I'm always sure of my job, and that's quite a lot!"

"You're always sure of your job, hey?" bawls Alex. "That's the slogan of the quitter! 'I'm gettin' my little old salary fifty-two weeks a year, and that's good enough for me.' That's the motto of the loser." With that he jumps up and sticks his face so close to Jared I thought he was gonna bite him or the like. "What about the future?" he hollers. "You must have brains, or you couldn't of collected that mass of junk in your dome. You got a million dollars' worth of salable stuff from the top of your collar to the crown of your derby and you're peddlin' it away for thirty-five a week. I'll bet right now you could produce a scheme for gettin' a quarter that would be unbeatable, legitimate, and successful. But if you was asked to dope out a scheme for gettin' twenty-five thousand dollars, the size of the figures alone would knock that thinker of yours cold! You can't think that big. Your mind's all cluttered up with little things. It's a junk pile. The same concentration and perseverance on some one *big* thing would put you over—and if you don't believe it, ask your boob boss, which undoubtedly did just that and is now keepin' you!"

"That's all rot!" remarks Jared. "There's about one chance in a million of getting over in New York. You've got to get in right, and even then it's largely a matter of luck! If I was ever asked, I'd tell every young man to keep away from New York. The town's too big! It swallows you up and you're buried there till—"

Zam!!! Alex bounces outa his chair and shakes his finger under Jared's nose.

"That's not true!" he hollers. "Listen to me, young feller! I came here a short time ago with one-tenth of the ability that you got. New York looked as cold and hard to me as it does to any rube that slinks in from the outlands, crazy with the desire to capture it. But instead of drivin' me back to the dear old farm, the tough conditions here *attracted* me. That is, takin' for granted your statement that they are tough, which I don't believe. I know that a man with the genuine goods can deliver them here at top price quicker than any other place on earth."

"But wait!" interrupts Jared, seemin' to catch some of Alex's pep. "Your case was exceptional. You must admit—"

"I don't admit nothin'!" roars Alex. "Suppose your argument is true. Let's say the chances for success here *are* slim. All right, fine! That's what made *me* stick! Your own argument makes New York *the* place to make good in. If there's satisfaction in winnin' over one man or a thousand, think of a hard-won square victory over six millions! Why, boy, the very quality of the competition here keeps a man on his toes and, if he makes good *here*, he's *done* somethin'!"

Well, believe me, when Alex wound up that speech they was so much pep in the room I felt like goin' out and tellin' Rockefeller I'd forgot more about the oil game than he ever knew! Jared looks kinda dazed and Alex never gives him a chance to get set.

"How about—ah—Miss Evans?" he says; "have you thought about her?"

"See here!" busts out Jared. "We won't discuss Mab—er—Miss Evans."

Alex grins.

"That's fine!" he says. "I'm glad you got some spirit left; they's hope for you yet! Let's see," he goes on, like they had been no interruption at all, "how long have you known Miss Evans?"

"Over a year," says Jared. "But I don't see what—"

Alex points a finger at him.

"You love her, don't you?" he barks out.

"Of course I do!" mumbles Jared, like he's answering without knowin' it.

"Then why don't you marry her?"

126

Jared stares at him like he's in a trance.

"*Marry* her?" he gasps. "Marry her? Why if I ever asked her *that*, she wouldn't even let me call on her any more!"

"You're crazy!" remarks Alex pleasantly. "Now listen, son! You been goin' around with that girl over a year, and if she didn't reciprocate your feelin' for her, you wouldn't of lasted that long. Jared, old boy, a year is too long to monopolize a girl without declarin' yourself! You're spoilin' her chances, and it's dead wrong! They is plenty of other young men which would give their left eye to take her to the movies and the like, but they're layin' off because, havin' always seen her with you, they take it for granted they is no chance. That's fine right now for both of you; but if anything should arise that would make you two part, it won't be as easy for her to replace you. Now you need a incentive, and a strong one, to put you across. They is no bigger incentive on earth than matrimony. Go to her and ask—"

"One minute!" butts in Jared. "I never was talked to like this in my life before, and why I'm permitting you to discuss my personal affairs, I don't know. As long as I am, I'll go through with it. What you say may be true, but this girl is different, and—"

"Jared," says Alex, "I don't doubt that she's different, but, nevertheless, she's a member of the well-known female sex, and I'm basin' my dope on that! I'll tell you what I'll do with you. You ask Miss Evans to marry you, and, if she refuses, I'll give you a job myself for fifty dollars a week; fifteen more than you get now. If she accepts, you gotta raise yourself by your own efforts to fifty dollars a week within six months, or go to work for me for twenty. Now if you got some red blood in you, let's see it!"

Well, Jared gets up and walks around the room for a minute and fin'ly he comes over and holds out his hand to Alex.

"You're on!" he says. "Only, I'll say this: If Mabel—er—Miss Evans, accepts me, I'll be so happy that I won't be good for *anything* for a month. If she refuses me, I'll *never* be any good any more! However, I'll try it. Perhaps I've been asleep. I don't know. But if this girl ever marries me—" He stops and bangs his fists on the table. "Oh, boy!!!!" he winds up.

Just then they is a ring at the telephone. The maid makes a entrance and claims Mr. Jared Rushton is wanted. In about five minutes, Jared comes back and apologizes.

"My boss, Mr. Hamilton," he says. "I've always got to let him know where he can get in touch with me after office hours. I gave him your phone number before I came here to-night." He turns to Alex. "That's what it is to be a valuable man," he says. "The boss wants me to get all the data together for an estimate on one of the biggest contracts we've ever had a whack at. That means I'll be up all night, so I'll have to leave now. Our four big contract experts are scattered 'round the country and the boss will have to go after this one himself to-morrow. There will be a conference at the Hotel Dubois, and—"

Alex jumps up, his eyes flashin'.

"Why can't *you* go after that contract?" he shoots out.

Jared looks like he's been hit on the chin.

"*Me?*" he stammers. "Why—why—"

"Why, why, nothin'!" butts in Alex. "Here's a chance for you to show Miss Evans, your boss, and the rest of the world what's in you. If your boss calls on you for the figures in this thing, then you must know more about it than he does, or anybody else in the office. Can you get him on the phone?"

"But—but I have never sold anything in my life!" says Jared. "You don't understand this thing at all. It requires experience and—oh, it's silly to even think of it! Why—"

"Yeh?" butts in Alex. "What's his number?" He rushes to the phone.

"Say, listen—please!" pleads Jared; "it's not a bit regular and—why, he'd fire me out of hand if I ever did anything like this!"

"The number!" bawls Alex, with the receiver off the hook.

"Riverside 33,312," stammers Jared, wringin' his hands. "But look here, you mustn't—"

Alex gets the number and Jared falls back in a chair, and mutters somethin' about bein' ruined for life. In another minute, Alex is announcin' to somebody that Mr. Jared Rushton wishes to speak to Mr. Hamilton on a matter of the greatest importance. Jared lets forth a wail like a dyin' fish or the like, and then Alex grabs him by the arms.

"Now, go to it!" he says. "Tell him you want a chance at this contract yourself. Say you know more about it than anyone else and have been plannin' the thing for weeks. You don't *think* you can land this contract—you *know* it!"

"But," wails Jared, "I *don't* know—"

Alex shoves him over to the phone.

Well, the funniest conversation you, I, or anybody else ever heard begins right then and there. Jared starts off kinda weak and tremblin' and I felt sorry for him, because from his answers it looked like a cinch that he was fired. Pretty soon he gets a little stronger, and in a few minutes he was talkin' like the boss was workin' for *him*! The only way I can figure it is that Alex had hopped him up so much that he got to where he believed himself that he was the only man on earth that could land this contract. When Jared says if he don't get this chance he's gonna quit his job right then and there and the boss can look elsewhere for the estimate figures, I almost fell off the couch, and Alex does a war dance.

Bang! Jared slams down the receiver and swings around on Alex.

"Well," he snaps out, "you've done it! I am to be at the Hotel Dubois at eleven to-morrow to meet the representatives of one of the biggest steel concerns in the country. I'm to take from them a contract running into millions. If I don't get it, I'm fired. If I do get it—well, there's no use talking about that part of it, because I won't!"

With that he sinks into a chair and buries his head in his hands. Alex keeps right on top of him.

"Fine!" he says, rubbin' his hands together. "Now call up Miss Evans and ask her to marry you!"

"What?" shrieks Jared, bouncin' up from his chair. "What is this? A nightmare? You've already probably cost me my job, and now you want to wreck my happiness! I was a fool to listen to you. I—"

"Sure!" says Alex. "Let's get her on the phone right away."

Jared looks wildly around the room and grabs for his hat. Alex pushes him back in a chair.

"Now, you listen to me!" he snarls, all the grin gone from him. "You are at this minute facin' the biggest thing that's ever come into your thirty-five-dollar-a-week life. You got a chance now to rise above the mob. You also got a chance to marry what is the greatest girl in the world, accordin' to your own admission. If you ask her to marry you *before* you go after this contract and she accepts you, think of the confidence you'll have! Why, boy, if this girl says she'll marry you, they ain't nothin' in New York can stop you from goin' over the top! Go on! You're all worked up now—go to it before you get cold!"

Jared grabs up the phone receiver, pale as a ghost.

"By heavens!" he says. "I—you—if—Gimme Morningside 77,638, quick!"

Alex closes the door and pulls me into the other room.

"That there's gonna be private," he says.

"Where did you meet this Miss Evans?" I says.

"H'mph!" grunts Alex. "I never seen the girl in my life! Jared simply told me about her, that's all!"

"Well," I says, "you certainly have balled things up. They ain't a doubt in my mind but that you've made that poor boy lose his job; and as far as I can see you're gonna make him lose his girl, too! I'd hate to be you when he staggers away from that phone!"

"Yeh?" grins Alex. "Well, I'll tell you somethin': As long as I'm goin' to all this trouble, I might as well get somethin' outta it. I'll bet you ten thousand to five the girl marries him and he lands the contract. If he loses either one, or both, you win!"

"Write it!" I says.

He hain't no more than handed the thing over to me, when in comes Jared. His face is all flushed and he acts like a guy walkin' in his sleep.

"I know neither of you will believe it," he says, in a far-away voice. "In fact, I think I'm dreaming, myself!"

"What did she say?" demands Alex, shakin' him.

"She said yes!" hollers Jared, in a voice that must of woke up sleepers in Kansas City. "Let me have my hat, I want to go over to her right away!"

"Well, what do you think of my dope now, hey?" says Alex.

"I'll never be able to thank you for what you've done for me!" says Jared, holdin' out his hand. "Why, just imagine! This wonderful girl is going to be my wife and I had no more idea—Why, this girl is as different from any other as—But you wouldn't understand—"

"I understand perfect!" says Alex, shakin' his hand. "And now the next thing is that contract, which should be a cinch for you after what you just done. Go over and see her now, but don't forget them figures on the—"

"Contract?" butts in Jared, jammin' on his hat. "What's a contract to me now? I'm going to marry the greatest girl in the world, man! Can you imagine her accepting me! Oh, boy!!!!!"

With that he does a few little fancy steps around the room, throwing a twenty-dollar pillow at Alex and a book at me.

This here's a new angle, and Alex grabs him.

"Look here!" he says. "I know you're in a hurry, so I don't want to hold you up now; but you wanna recover from this here till you land that contract! You'll lose your job if you don't, and you ain't gonna start off married life outta work, are you?"

"I should worry!" sings Jared, still one-steppin' about the room. "I can get another job—forty of 'em! I can get anything at all, now. She's going to marry me, she's going to marry me!"

He dashes for the door, and Alex runs after him.

"What time is the appointment with the big steel men?" he shrieks in his ear.

"What's a big steel man to me?" asks Jared, struggling to get away. "What's anything? I'll bet she would have accepted me long ago if—"

"What time is that conference?" howls Alex.

"I care not!" sings Jared, throwing the phone book up in the air, and a idiotic grin at me. "I'm going to have a quiet wedding and—"

I thought Alex was gonna choke him!

"She's going to marry me, she's going to marry me!"

Personally, I developed a bad case of the hystericals.

"The time?" screams Alex.

"Eleven o'clock," says Jared.

"Will you promise me on your word of honor to meet me at that hotel at ten to-morrow, in view of what I done for you?" says Alex.

"Sure!" hollers Jared. "I'll promise anything! Look what's been promised to me!"

With that he breaks away from Alex and dives out the door.

Alex comes back and sinks down into a chair, wipin' off his fevered brow with a handkerchief.

"That baby is a plain nut!" I remarks.

"Whew!" pants Alex. "I started somethin' now, that's sure! Still, I don't blame the boy. I felt the same way when Eve claimed she'd wed me, and I guess you did too when Alice went temporarily insane and brung you into the family. If I can keep him keyed up to that pitch to-morrow, he'll land that contract, and I'll land your five thousand!"

"He won't land nothin'!" I says. "He's gone nutty now, and you'll be lucky if he shows up at all. This here's *one* bet I win!"

"Yeh?" snaps Alex, gettin' up and reachin' for his hat. "D'ye wanna take five thousand more of it?"

"No!" I says. "Good night!"

At nine forty-five the next mornin', which is practically the middle of the night for me, Alex comes around and drags me outta bed. He says he's goin' down and watch Jared put the contract over and he wants me along to witness the losin' of my bet.

We are in the lobby of the hotel gettin' ready to have Jared paged, when along he comes with some dame he must have kidnapped from the Follies when Ziegfield was busy countin' up the receipts or somethin'. I'll tell the world fair she was *some* girl.

She's lookin' at Jared like he was the eleventh wonder of the world, and he's gazin' back at her like she was the other ten.

"Hello!" hollers Alex, grabbin' Jared's hand and makin' believe it's a pump handle. "Congratulations! I wish I felt as happy as both you folks look!"

"You couldn't!" says Jared, still with that dazed look on his face. "This is my future wife, gentlemen. We're on our way down for the license now. Come on along as witnesses. We're going to be married right—"

"What about that steel contract?" Alex butts in. "Did you get the figures all together last night?"

"I did not!" says Jared. "What do I care about a steel contract? I landed a bigger contract than that, and—"

"Pardon me," interrupts the girl, with her million-dollar smile. "What is this contract regarding the steel?"

Alex tells her the whole dope from start to finish, and when he gets through the girl turns to Jared and says the followin':

"Well, dear, I suppose this horrid old business could wait, but just run up and land that contract for a—a—wedding gift for me! It shouldn't take you very long. I'll wait here for you."

Oh, boy!!! Talkin' about "just runnin' up and landin'" a million-dollar contract like she was sendin' him for stamps or the like!

"All right, honey," says Jared; "I'll be down in five minutes!"

They was *fifteen* minutes partin'.

Alex and Jared and I got in the elevator, and on the way up Jared talked about nothin' else but his comin' marriage. When Alex tried to butt in and ask regardin' the estimate for this steel job, Jared gets peevish and says that will be a cinch and is practically over with; but what's worryin' him is the best place to go for a honeymoon!

We are met at the door of the room by a little bald-headed guy, and Jared introduces himself. The little guy looks at us and says he presumes we are Jared's associates—whatever that is. Before Jared can deny the charge, Alex presents him with a kick on the shins and says we are all of that.

Inside, they is a long table and four more guys sittin' at it. They all look like Wall Street and large money, and the table is covered with papers. Jared sits down and begins hummin' "Here Comes the Bride," and we sit down beside him. One guy gets up and says they have talked with five big contractors already, and they ain't made up their mind which bid to accept. If Jared can show them somethin' better than they've seen, the order is all his. Jared pulls out his watch and gets up.

"Gentlemen," he says, "I have an appointment with my future wife in five minutes. I will be on time! I don't know what these other fellows have offered to do for you, but I'll say this: We can erect your plant for exactly $1,789,451.92. That's our lowest price, and if we talked all day I couldn't take off a cent! My concern is known all over the country for the sterling quality of workmanship and materials it employs on every job, whether it's the erection of a lamp post or a city—and we've done both! We will be pleased to list you among the thousands of our satisfied patrons."

With that he reaches for his hat and would of been out of the door, if Alex hadn't held him back with a look.

"But," says one guy, "your figures are more than ten thousand dollars over your nearest competitor's. How about that?"

Jared is starin' out the window.

"I figure we can get a nice flat in the Bronx for about eighty a month," he says, half to himself. "What do you pay?" he finishes, turnin' to Alex.

Alex says nothin', and the five guys look at each other kinda funny.

"When could your firm begin work?" asks one of them.

"Immediately!" says Jared. "I'm going to use your phone here for a minute and telephone my future wife. She's downstairs waiting and will be worried sick—I said I'd be right back!" He walks across the room, while them guys all stare after him like they're in a trance themselves. "Still," mutters Jared, "she mightn't like to live in the Bronx at that!"

While he's on the phone, the five guys puts their heads together and has a whispered conference. By the time he's finished, so are they.

"Mr. Rushton," says the little guy, gettin' up and clearin' his throat, "we have decided to give you the contract. Your methods of salesmanship are somewhat unusual—but they may be due to your extreme confidence, which anybody can see is the right kind of stuff in that line and—"

The little guy goes on with a lot of talk about figures, to which Alex and me listens respectfully and Jared don't listen at all. And fin'ly the little guy says again that they're gonna give Jared the contract, and mebbe, if his future wife is waiting—

"Thanks!" says Jared. "She *is* waiting and—"

"Shall we draw up the contract now?" butts in Alex. "They's a notary on this floor."

In half a hour we are down in the lobby again, havin' had to hold Jared by main force long enough to sign this thing. The first guy we bump into is his boss!

"Where have *you* been?" he hollers at Jared. "I suppose you've botched everything all up. I'll be the laughing stock of New York! Where are those figures for that steel contract?"

Jared looks at him for a minute like, Who is this person? Then he reaches into his pocket and pulls out the contract.

"Here's your old contract!" he says. "I'm going to take a month off. I'm going to get married. When I come back I want seventy-five dollars a week to start and a job as head of the contract department. And, also—don't never yell at me like that again."

I thought his boss would die of apoplexy then and there. He stares at Jared, snatches the contract, reads a few lines—and then I got the idea he was gonna kiss all of us!

"My boy, you're a wonder!" he says. "I always knew you had the stuff in you! I'll discuss—the—er—the matter of your salary when you come back."

"We'll finish it right now!" butts in Jared. "I don't want nothing worrying me while I'm on my honeymoon. Do I get that or don't I?"

"But," stammers the boss, "your commission on that contract alone will run—"

"Yes or no!" says Jared very cold.

"Yes!" says the boss, with a sigh that could be heard in Harlem. "No wonder you landed that contract if you went after them that way! I've been asleep!"

"No," says Jared, "I've been doing the dreaming."

CHAPTER VII

ART IS WRONG

Every time some guy goes over the top to notoriety and money in this movie called life, they is some 5,678,954 also rans which wags their heads from side to side and says, "Well—no wonder. He was born that way and couldn't help himself!" Then, they go back to their dub jobs and wish they was lucky.

That stuff is all wrong! A guy may be born with different color hair from the next guy, but he's never born with any secret of success that the kid in the adjoinin' crib ain't got. All you need to be born with in order to get the world familiar with your last name is the usual number of arms, legs and etc. and a mad habitual yearnin' to make good that a sudden hypodermic of success don't kill. Anything but failure is possible to a hustler, and by a hustler I don't mean one of them breezy birds which makes a lotta noise, thinks they is only one letter in the alphabet and that's the one after "H," but the guy which takes setbacks as encouragement and quits tryin' the day the undertaker is called in.

They's many a big artist whose ancestors thought paint was used for the sides of barns only, they's many a famous actor whose father figured Shakespeare was the name of a puddin', they's many a big league author come from families which confined their readin' matter to the city directory, and so it goes all along the line— Columbus's old man was a cotton picker. You don't inherit success, you take it by force, usin' your ambition, nerve and ability as the weapons.

The above information was handed on to me by Alex. He says Broadway is too narrow and Vermont moonlight had it lookin' dark at night and he then proceeds to wed one of the prettiest girls that ever looked over the Winter Garden footlights—she makes homemade bread now, too! The first time he went to the Metropolitan Opera House he claims he'd like grand opera if they wouldn't sing and when does the acrobats come out, yet the next week he's able to take a apartment on Riverside Drive. This here is just a few of the things Alex done to break up the dull monotony of life in a burg where that and death is mere incidents.

The wife and I is sittin' together in the parlor one night and she's knittin' a sweater for me that will prob'ly make me off her for life, whilst I'm readin' aloud to her from the only novel in which true love and the like don't win out in the end. It's called "Simpson's Universal Educator" and the subject we are on is how wet is the Pacific, or some such hot stuff as that. They is a ring at the bell and the wife grabs the book outa my hand and slings about thirty dollars' worth of wool over my arms.

"Sit up straight," she says, "and look interested in this! You're helpin' me knit—get that? Look as if you like it and the minute the door opens call me dear."

"What's the idea?" I says, sittin' there with my arms out straight and stiff before me like a doll or the like. "I don't get—"

"Sssh!" she whispers. "That's probably Ruth Hopper and her husband. She's trying to get him to quit playing pinochle all night and she wants to show him what a ideal husband does."

"A pinochle fiend, hey?" I says. "Well, lead him on! We got a little game down at the corner and he'll just make up the set. It's gettin' around time for me to leave anyways. I been in a half hour now and—"

Well, at that moment our charmin' maid leads in no less than Alex and his wife Eve. Speakin' of good lookers, this dame would make Morgan forget about Wall Street, and she's wearin' a dress that must of put some Fifth Avenue store over. But the wife begins bein' pleasant to gaze upon and a delight to the naked eye where Eve leaves off. Why, she's got a movie contract which she holds over my head every time I stay out till ten o'clock and the like. Them two dames in the one room is more than the average guy can stand and how they ever come to fall for a coupla guys like me and Alex is a subject for bigger brains than mine. They say women is peculiar, hey? Well, it's a good thing for the average guy that they are!

She's knittin' a sweater for me that will prob'ly make me off her for life.

"Well!" remarks Eve, lookin' from me to the wife. "How perfectly sweet! If you two only knew what a pretty picture you make!"

"How perfectly sweet! If you two only knew what pretty picture you make!"

"Yeh," I says, gettin' up and dumpin' the near sweater on the table. "You'd almost think we wasn't married, hey?"

"Speaking of pictures," says the wife, allowin' Alex to kiss her—a thing I loathe, "let's all go down and see 'Wronged By Mistake.' They tell me—"

"Nothin' stirrin'," I butts in. "I wanna see Beryldine Nearer in 'The Woman Which Lost.' She's some dame, believe me! If I was the leadin' man in her pictures I'd work for nothin'."

"Is that so?" says the wife, her voice as cold as Cape Nome. "Why didn't you marry her then instead of me?"

"She didn't ask me till it was too late," I says, grinnin' like a wolf.

"Here, here!" says Alex. "How is it you people is always quarrelin' every time I come here for a visit?"

"We figure you'll get sore and beat it," I says.

"Now, boys," says Eve, "let's forget we are all one family and be friends. Why aren't you folks out celebratin' peace to-night?"

"We wasn't invited," I says. "And I have bought my last ticket from a speculator."

"Invited?" says Eve, which always takes everything except Alex serious. "Why, all New York seems to be on Broadway!"

"That's what people from Chicago always thinks," I says. "But they's more to the town than that."

"Oh, hush that near comedy," says the wife. "C'mon, we're going to see 'Wronged By Mistake.'"

"I'll see Beryldine Nearer," I says in a loud and angry voice, "or we don't go nowhere!"

We went to see "Wronged By Mistake."

The movin' picture company which is responsible for this film claims it cost them $100,000 to make the picture. Maybe it did, I don't know. What I do know is that it cost me $1000 to see it! Why? Lend me your ears, as the dumb guy said.

The hero of this here picture was no less than Carrington De Vire. This guy's name is familiar in burgs where they don't know if Wilson or Washington is still president of the United States. His name is on more collars than you ever seen and he gets more money a week than you and me makes in six years, even if you cut his advertised salary in half. He's prob'ly caused more girls to take their pens in hand than any massage cream in the world and to say he is a handsome dog is like remarkin' that the Grand Canyon is pleasant to look at. The only magazine which ain't printed his photo at least once with a auto, a country place and a coupla trick dogs at his side is the *Hardware Trade Review* and the *Steamfitters' Friend*.

The minute Carrington De Vire appears on the screen and gives the natives a treat by presentin' one and all with a pleasant smile, the wife and Eve begins to rave about him out loud. He kisses the leadin' woman and they let forth a sigh which would of made me jealous only I got too much brains. The villain slams him, prob'ly because he got sick of lookin' at the big fathead, and the women groans. He knocks the villain kickin' and they applaud their hands off and when he fights his way through a gang of supes which will lose their jobs if they don't fall when he hits 'em, I thought most of the female part of the audience would pass away with joy!

"I think he's simply wonderful, don't you?" murmurs Eve to the wife.

They is no argument about it.

Alex give a snort.

"If they's anything wonderful about that feller," he says, "then I'm more astonishin' than wireless. Anybody can do that stuff! Why—"

"Why, the idea!" butts in Eve. "I actually believe you're jealous. I think Carrington De Vire is simply divine—marvelous!"

"Wait till you see Niagara Falls," I says.

"Both of them are jealous," says the wife. "I'm surprised at Alex saying that any one could act as well as Carrington De Vire. Why, I think he's got Faversham beaten a mile. You have to be born with talent like that!"

"I think the wife's right in one thing at last," I says. "I like them male movie heroes and carbolic acid the same way, but you got to hand it to this bird—he's *some* actor! Yep, Alex, you can't learn that stuff out of no book, you gotta be born with it."

"You're all crazy!" announces Alex, with another snort. "I can go out right now and dig up a dozen fellers which never seen a camera in their life and they'll duplicate anything Carrington De Vire ever did on a screen. Where does he get off to be wonderful? Some feller with brains writes a play, another feller with money puts it on and then another feller with technical knowledge tells De Vire, which ain't got none of them things, where to stand and the like while he acts it. Why—"

"Ridiculous!" butts in Eve. "Carrington De Vire has extraordinary talent. He has thousands of admirers all over the country. Why— why—he's famous!"

"Of course," says the wife. "It's too silly to talk about. Alex has reached the stage now where he thinks he can do anything!"

"Yeh?" says Alex. "Well, I reached the stage where I thought I could do anything about three minutes after I was born! I'll bet right now I can go down to the docks or some place and get a handsome stevedore and make him as big a star as Carrington De Vire in six months!"

"Don't be idiotic," laughs Eve. "Imagine a stevedore as a moving picture star!"

"Why not?" demands Alex, lookin' like the idea had made a hit with him. "Ain't a stevedore as good as anybody else? I'll bet a thousand dollars even that I can catch one or somebody like him and make him a movie star. What d'ye say?"

"I'll say this," I says. "We come here to see this picture and not to hear you make a speech. This here's a theatre and not no race track and forget about that bettin' thing. If you can make a movie star out of a stevedore, I can make a watch outa a hard boiled egg!"

They is some people behind us which can't see the picture on account of us talkin' and they begin to hiss at us. It bothers Alex the same as rain worries a duck.

"Is they steam escapin' somewheres?" he remarks, turnin' his head. "Why, brakemen have became railroad presidents," he goes on, "bootblacks have became bankers, prize fighters have turned evangelists and the United States has went dry. Why shouldn't a stevedore become a movie star?"

"We'll all become throwed outa here if you don't keep quiet!" I says.

"Ssh, Alex," says the wife. "Don't get so excited about it. There's no use attempting the impossible and—"

"They ain't nothin impossible!" butts in Alex. "I'm willin' to prove it. Why don't somebody bet me, hey?"

"Why don't you hire Madison Square Garden for that speech?" hisses a guy behind us. "Heavens, what a pest!"

"Call the usher," puts in a dame with him. "Them people has did nothin' but talk since they come in here!"

"What d'ye want us to do—sing?" growls Alex.

"Alex, be still!" whispers Eve. "I've missed the whole picture through your talking. Now we'll have to stay and see it all over again."

"Have a nice time," says Alex, gettin' up and grabbin' my arm. "We'll wait outside for you. One dose a day of Carrington De Vire is all I can take!"

The bunch in back glares at us and says somethin' about what a crime it is to let drunken men come into a theatre.

Outside on the pavement, Alex lets forth a snort and whiffs the fresh air like it was wine.

"Think of my wife sittin' in there and worshippin' that big stiff," he snarls. "And yours, too!"

"We all have our faults," I says. "I knowed a guy once which was crazy over fried parsnips."

"They ain't nothin' to laugh at in this," he says, slappin' his hands together. "I ain't a jealous man, but no movie hero is gonna be no god to my wife!"

"Why don't you go in the movies yourself, then?" I says. "They might hire you for a picture with Carrington De Vire in it, and you can knock him kickin' in five reels or the like."

"Huh!" says Alex, "what do I care about the movies? I got a better plan than that and it will accomplish the same purpose. I'll show Eve and the rest of you how easy it is to be a movie hero—I'll make money out of it, too!" he adds, with the old glitter in his eyes.

"What are you gonna do?" I says. "Speak quick, I can't stand excitement!"

For answer he takes me into the hotel across the street and leads me into the writin' room. He sits down and writes on a piece of paper for a minute and then he hands it to me.

"Cast your eyes over that," he says, "and if it's satisfactory—sign it!"

This is what I read,

"I, Alex Hanley, agree to hire one handsome, tall and perfectly built stevedore, longshoreman, truck driver or some one engaged in a equally honest profession, one who has never appeared before a camera or upon any stage and who has no knowledge of theatricals, and within six months from date to make him a full fledged, acknowledged star of the moving pictures.

"In the event of said undertaking being successful, the undersigned agrees to pay Alex Hanley one thousand dollars. In the event of failure, Alex Hanley agrees to forfeit the same sum."

I handed it back to him.

"Listen!" I says. "Don't be a nut *all* your life. You got as much chance of—"

"Did you ever see me fall down on anything?" he butts in, dippin' a pen in the ink and handin' it to me.

"Not even a banana peel," I admits. "But they is a limit to everything—even the war's over. In the first place, even if you could do this, it would cost you more than a thousand dollars and—"

"Leave that to me," he says, pushin' over the pen. "And sign here!"

"But—" I says.

"Hurry up, the ink will be dry," he cuts me off.

I give in.

"Alex," I says. "This is a crime! If I ever win one bet in my life, I'll win this one. You'll make a movie star outa a stevedore, hey? Why —"

"Want a thousand more?" he grins pleasantly.

"No!" I hollers. "Let's go over and meet the girls."

The search for the future king of the movies begins merrily the next day. I went with Alex to see that he didn't put nothin' over on me and at the end of the week he had dug up three promisin' leads. They was a plumber's helper which had a wonderful figure, but a scar on his cheek showed up in a snapshot Alex took of him and he was laid aside with a sigh. Then they was a waiter which was better lookin' than Mary Pickford, but a trifle stoop-shouldered. The third guy was hustlin' baggage at Grand Central Station and was a perfect Venus except for some missin' teeth which queered him when he smiled and what's a movie hero without a smile?

Well, I'm havin' the time of my life kiddin' Alex, when one day as we are walkin' along Third Avenue in search of his prey, he grabs me by the arm, yells, "I got him!" and starts across the street on the run. They is a big truck standin' there and a husky on the back of it is engaged in coaxin' pig iron off of it on to the street. He stood about six foot three without bein' shaved and weighed accordingly, all bone and muscle not countin' his head. He turns around and — Oh, boy!!!!

Say! I seen some good lookers in my time, male and female, but this baby had it on 'em all! His hair is that black, wavy kind that the cabaret hounds wish they had and he's got a skin like a week old baby. He must of painted his teeth with enamel twice a day and he's there with a pair of eyelashes that would make a chorus girl take carbolic. On the level, he's so handsome he don't look real — and that with all the signs of honest toil at the truck on him, too! Alex taps him on the shoulder and he swings around.

"What's yours?" he growls.

"I have come to make your fortune," announces Alex with a grin. Then he turns to me. "Ain't he a peach, hey?" he says.

The big guy drops the pig iron and looks from Alex to me.

"What kinda stuff is this?" he growls. "What d'ye mean I'm a peach?"

"You are the luckiest man in New York," says Alex. "I have come to make you famous and rich!"

The big guy grins.

"Listen!" he says. "They're awful tough on hop fiends in this burg now and they'll be a copper along in a minute, so you better duck. I know you guys is no less than J. P. Morgan and John D. Rockefeller, if not more, and you'll gimme a million dollars in nickels if I'll tell you where to get a layout. But I ain't got the time, I gotta get this stuff off here and—"

With that he turns around and goes to work again.

"Drop that iron!" says Alex. "You'll never soil your hands with manual labor again."

"Hey!" snarls the big guy. "Git away, will you? I always feel sorry for you dope fiends, but if you guys don't lay off me, I'll bounce the two of you. Now, beat it!"

"Well," I says to Alex, "he's ignorant anyways. We got that part all settled and—"

"Look here!" says Alex, darin'ly grabbin' the big guy by the arm. "We're neither dope fiends nor maniacs. I want to ask you a few questions and, if your answers suit me, I'll hire you for a hundred dollars a week to do special work for me. To show you I'm not foolin', take this for your trouble whether we do business or not."

With that he hands him a twenty dollar bill.

"Aha!" yells the big guy. "Coupla counterfeiters, hey?" He snatches the bill and grabs Alex. "So you guys want me to pass this for you—I got it!" He starts to drag Alex along the pavement and half Third Avenue stops to watch it. "I'll git a reward for this!" I heard him mutter.

Alex throws him off—he's stronger than he looks.

"You better not take that head of yours into no pool room," he snarls, "or somebody'll get two billiard balls and play with it for a set. Take your hands off me and listen. That bill is as good as the inside of a church. C'mon into this store and I'll prove it!"

They's somethin' about Alex that makes this guy hesitate, and Alex pulls him into a cigar store, whilst I shoo away the disappointed crowd which looked for manslaughter at least.

In a minute they come out. The big guy has twenty single bills in his hand and a dazed look on his face. Alex is grinnin'.

"Now are you satisfied?" says Alex.

The big guy shoves the dough in his overalls.

"The sugar seems O.K.," he says. "Say! I gotta work a week for that much dough, so I might as well give you five minutes of my time. What's the idea, hey?"

"Now, Delancey Calhoun," says Alex, "how would you—"

"Wait a minute!" grins the other guy. "I knowed they was a ball up somewheres. Where d'ye get that Calhoun stuff? My name's Tim O'Toole."

"Not no more!" says Alex, returnin' the grin. "From now on it's Delancey Calhoun—get that?"

"A nut is a funny thing," says O'Toole, pressin' the dough in his pocket. "But—sure, I'm Delancey Calhoun! That's a swell name at that—it sounds like a Lenox Avenue apartment house. What d'ye want me to do, outside of that?"

"How would you like to be a actor?" says Alex.

"Nothin' doin'!" says Delancey. "I got a steady job and I'm too fond of eatin'."

"Don't be a fool!" says Alex. "That stuff about actors not eatin' regular is a thing of the past. These days a actor makes more money than a banker. Did you ever appear on the stage anywheres in your life?"

"I did not!" snarls Delancey. "And I can lick the guy which claims I did!"

"Fine!" says Alex, lookin' at me. "Now of course you've seen movin' pictures, hey?"

"Sure!" says Delancey. "What d'ye think I am—ig'rant?"

"Not at all," says Alex. "Do you think if you had a chance and was well paid for it, you could do the things them heroes does in the movies?"

Delancey Calhoun, née Tim O'Toole, throws out his chest from here to South Dakota.

"Do I *think* so?" he says. "Why, say, pal—that stuff would be soft for me! I ain't no second Mary Pickford or the like and Chaplin might grab off more laughs to the reel than me, but when it come to this here cowboy and full dress stuff—Oh, lady!!!"

"You're hired!" hollers Alex, slappin' him on the back. "Startin' right now your salary is a hundred a week. Drive that truck back to where it belongs and throw up your job."

"A hundred a week, hey?" says Delancey, rollin' his eyes. "Oh, lady!! In a month I'll have Carnegie gnashin' his teeth!" He breaks off and swings around on Alex. "Look here!" he says, "I been drivin' this truck for two years. I got a good steady job from eight in the mornin' till ten at night, and I get twenty berries a week for it. I don't know nothin' about this nut job of yours, but if I don't get my hundred every week—well, they's gonna be a funeral with you bein' featured in it, get that?"

"That's all right," says Alex. "I'll deposit your first six months' salary in the bank for you—how's that?"

"What could be sweeter?" says Delancey. "They's just one other thing."

"Speak up!" says Alex.

"As long as I'm gonna be a movie actor," says Delancey, "do I get a dress suit to wear?"

"Sure!" says Alex. "Why?"

"Well," grins Delancey, "I never had one of them open faced suits on in me life and in fact I was savin' up to get one now. I'm simply nutty to put on one of them layouts and knock the innocent onlookers silly. If you hit a tough week, I might take ninety-five bucks and let the rest go over a few days, but I gotta have the dress suit and that goes!"

"It's yours," says Alex, diggin' me in the ribs.

"All right," says Delancey, "I'll go down now and make the boss faint by quittin'. I'll meet you anywheres you says to-morrow."

"You will not," says Alex. "I'll ride right down on that truck with you now!"

About two weeks later, Alex comes up to the flat and tells me to put on my hat and cane. He says he's gonna take me over to the studio and show me Delancey Calhoun's first picture.

"So you're really goin' through with it, hey?" I says. "What company did you get him landed with?"

"The Par-Excellence Feature Film Company," he says.

"I never heard tell of it," I says. "Who's in back of it?"

"A young feller by the name of Alex Hanley!" he comes back, grinnin'.

"What?" I hollers. "D'ye mean to say you started a movie foundry to put this guy over?"

"I'll leave it to you," he tells me, "when we get to the studio. Let's go!"

On the way over he shows me a lot of the advertisin' copy with which he's gonna introduce Delancy Calhoun to the waitin' world. I must say it was hot stuff! It claims that Delancey Calhoun is the sole heir to the $20,000,000 left by the late Artemus Calhoun which died twenty years ago. The will was given to his lawyers, Sandringham, Bellew and Fitch, with instructions not to open it for twenty years. When it was opened, it was found that them twenty millions was left to his only nephew, Delancey. Alex has opened a law office downtown under the name of Sandringham, Bellew and Fitch, so's to take care of the reporters and other guys of a inquisitive nature. Then comes the kick.

Delancey, a handsome and accomplished young giant, is tired of the "sham and deceit" of his own "exalted social set" and it's his ambition to wed a girl of the common people and let her enjoy some of the millions his hard-fisted uncle wrung from their toil. He also has another aim in life and that is to accomplish a sweepin' reform of the movie game. He's always been a great fan himself, but he's sick of the impossible plays which has been foisted on a innocent and nickel spendin' public. Therefore, he has organized his own movie company, will produce his own pictures from real life stories of the eternal struggle, and last but not least, he'll appear personally in them himself, to gratify a whim he's had since he first looked over the side of a cradle. He thinks the average movie hero is sickenin', and he wants to show the world how a real hero would act. He will appear in twelve pictures only. Each will be a episode in the greatest mystery story ever written entitled, "What was Hector's Choice?" Every single female in the country is invited to see this picture and send in their solution of the mystery. *The one that comes nearest to the correct answer will become the bride of Delancy Calhoun and his twenty million bucks.*

Oh, boy!!!

"Alex," I says, "I'll tell the world this is great stuff! It must be gonna cost you a bunch of money. Where do you get off?"

"Your head and glue is the two thickest things I ever seen," he says. "Where do I get mine, hey? I get it from the sale of the pictures this bird makes. In a coupla months they'll be riots in theatres all over the country to see this guy in the movies!"

"Maybe," I says. "But how are you gonna pull 'em in? Right off the bat he's gotta compete with Chaplin, Mary Pickford and the like."

"I didn't wanna spring my ace so soon on you," he says, "but I guess I got to. How am I gonna pull 'em in? This way—*single women will be admitted free at every theatre where this picture is shown!*"

Wheee!!!!

"You're there, Alex!" I admits. "But suppose the men and married women stays away?"

"Stays away?" he says. "They'll break their way in! The married women will wanna see Delancey and get a idea of what they missed, and the men will wanna see what this big fathead looks like, if only to kid him."

"What kind of a actor is he?" I says.

"Wait till you see him," says Alex. "He's got the studio standin' on its ear! He thinks he's the greatest actor the world ever seen and everybody else from the director to the camera men is dubs. He refuses to fake any of the fight scenes and I gotta pay supers ten bucks a day to take his wallops. The first time he had a love scene with the leadin' lady he thought it was on the level and went out and got a marriage license. He argued two hours in favor of real bullets for the duel he fights with the villain and refused to play a scene supposed to be in Alaska because the studio's in Jersey. He claims the guy which wrote the scenario escaped from a lunatic asylum and he plays the second two reels his own way. I've had three different casts work with him because he gets them all sore by his kiddin' them about art. He takes everything in dead earnest and tried to beat up the villain on the street twice because he's supposed to hate him in the picture. But—this first episode is *some* film!!!"

I seen the picture in the private projectin' room and Alex told the truth when he called it *"some* film." In fact that there would of been as good a title for the whole picture as the one they had. They was more adventures happened to Delancey Calhoun in them five reels than Robinson Crusoe, Columbus, Kit Carson and Davy Crockett had in their combined lives! He was a heart-breaker one second and a head-breaker the next. He had insisted to Alex that one villain wasn't enough for him to foil, so they had about a dozen and he trimmed 'em all. They was also several heroines for him to save and clasp on his manly bosom, which same he did in evenin' clothes only. It was nothin' for him to save a maiden in distress from a sinkin' ship and the next second appear in a lifeboat with a dress suit on, rowin' for shore. No matter if the scene was mornin' or night, Alaska or the Sahara Desert, Delancey was there in his little dress suit. He would of parted with that and his left eye with the same willingness.

Apart from the film itself, which might of been good or might of been bad, but certainly was excitin' for your life, Delancey was a riot! He was the handsomest thing I ever seen on a screen and I don't blame all the dames in the studio for fallin' for him. In that treasured dress suit of his which cost Alex as much as a limousine, they ain't no woman on earth that wouldn't get a thrill when she looked at him, provided he didn't start no conversation. He looked class— that's all they is to it!

When we come out from seein' the picture, Delancey is walkin' around the studio, still with the dress suit on. He's tellin' one of the best directors in the country how to properly produce a movie and said director is takin' it hard. He breaks off when he sees us.

"Hello!" he says. "Well, what d'ye think of me? I'm a knockout, hey?"

"Easily that," I admits, shakin' his hand. "How d'ye like bein' a actor?"

"Rotten!" he says. "This stuff is the bunk and them actors gimme a pain. I think they're all nutty. How they get money for this hop is past me! All I do all day is pretend I'm this and pretend I'm that and the foreman of this layout keeps yellin', 'Register fear!' and stuff like that at me. I don't know why this friend of yours is givin' me money for this, but I bet they's a catch to it somewheres!"

"Isn't he simply delicious?" says the leadin' woman, with a fond glance at Delancey.

"Delicious, hey?" he snorts. "What d'ye think I am—a pie?"

They is a vampire there and she turns up her nose.

"I think he's impossible!" she says. "He hasn't the slightest conception of art."

"Lemme alone!" growls Delancey. "I'm as good a actor as you guys is, if not better. Where d'ye get that art stuff?"

"Heavens!" says the vampire. "You must have worked all your life to acquire ignorance, for no one was ever *born* as stupid as you! All you have is your looks."

"Heavens!" says the vampire. "You must have worked a your life to acquire ignorance, for no one was ever *born* as stupid as you!"

"Yeh," snarls Delancey. "And all Rockefeller's got is a billion!"

At this point Alex stepped in and prevented bloodshed.

Well, Delancey is as big a success as a movie star as Boston is as a town, and within a month he's swept the country like a new dance. That stuff about him bein' a millionaire and willin' to marry the girl which guesses the answer to the mystery in "What Was Hector's Choice?" caught on with the ladies like cold cream and his handsome map did the rest. His picture is plastered all over the country and kids which barely knowed their A, B, C's, is familiar with his name. His mail arrives daily in freight cars and Alex had four guys workin' on nothin' but autographin' his photos for "A Admirer" and "Your Unknown Friend." Alex got a quarter the each for said photos to cover the "wrapping and mailing charges" and made a nice little profit on the side.

With all this success, though, Delancey Calhoun kept his head. He never appeared at no banquets, addressed meetin's on "The Future of the Motion Picture Industry," or as much as glanced at the daily slew of mail. When the dames around the studio cast languishin' glances at his handsome form, he glared at 'em like a infuriated turtle. If one of 'em remarked that it was a nice day by way of startin' a slight flirtation, Delancey would answer that he couldn't help it, and walk away. He never spent a nickel foolishly or at all, and when the auto agents swooped down on him, he borrowed cigars from them and beat it.

The most astonishin' thing, though, was the way he acted about the movies durin' his career as a star. He never stopped claimin' that the whole thing was the bunk and that it was idiotic for a grown person to put on a wig and take off the old banker or the like, when they was only a fifty buck a week actor. He insisted that anything as silly as the movies was could never last and they was more real money in the truckin' business for a man that knew the game as he did and had plenty of wagons. When Alex argues with him and says that many of the big stars makes fifty thousand a year, he tells Alex to stop usin' opium because it'll get him in the end.

At the end of three months, Delancey has made Alex pay him a percentage of the receipts and a salary of a thousand a week, but his opinion of the movie business is unchanged. He explains the fact that he's makin' plenty of money out of it by sayin' that Alex must be takin' it out of his own pocket and is simply makin' pictures to cover up his real game, which is prob'ly safe crackin'. Alex throws up his hands and lets him be after that one.

When the dames cast languishing glances at his handsome form, he glared at them like an infuriated turtle.

Fin'ly the last picture is made and Alex gives out the information to a expectant world that a girl in Brisbane, Australia, has won the guessin' contest and Delancey Calhoun's hand, and the famous star will sail immediately to wed her. The newspapers all prints pictures of 'em both, Alex gettin' the lucky dame's by photographin' his stenographer. A couple of papers didn't get neither and runs pictures of Brisbane, Australia, so's to be on the job anyways. Then Alex collects the thousand bucks I bet him that he couldn't make a movie star outa a truck driver and prepares to break the news to his wife and mine that he has done the same. He figures this will kill forever their wild infatuation for Carrington De Vire, the idol of the screen.

At that point, Delancey Calhoun walks into the office.

"Ah, Delancey," says Alex, "I was just gonna send for you. Now that our original contract has expired, let me congratulate you. You done great and far better than even I expected. You're famous the world over and must have a good sized bankroll if you've stayed in at nights and kept away from race tracks and the like. I only intended this as a experiment, but it has gone over so big that I want you to sit down here and sign a contract for five years at the biggest salary you ever heard of. We'll make the greatest pictures the world—"

"Wait a minute!" butts in Delancey. "Don't rave no more. My name is Tim O'Toole again and not Delancey, which sounds like a collar. I'm sick and tired of movin' pictures and that big salary stuff is as much bunk as the rest of it. I ain't goin' around rescuin' nutty dames, beatin' up supes which is supposed to be the desperate smugglers and divin' off bridges no more! I'm goin' to make a honest livin' and I've bought out the truckin' business I was workin' for when you come along and made a movie star and a simp outa me. I'll be takin' in money there long after the movies is gone and all the pictures I'll ever move from now on will be loaded on one of my wagons. Fare-thee-well, and I hope they's no hard feelings. If they is, I ain't gonna sob out loud over it!"

For a minute Alex was speechless. Then he comes to and works a hour tryin' to get the ex-Delancey Calhoun to change his mind. They was nothin' doin'. In fact, Delancey walked out and left us flat in the middle of Alex's wail.

Well, anyways, Alex still had one satisfaction left and that was to prove to Eve and the wife that he had put over a truck driver as a movie star. He done it after dinner that night and if he caused any sensation, I failed to see it with the naked eye.

"Well," says Eve, "that proves my argument."

"Proves *your* argument?" hollers Alex. "Didn't you claim movie stars was born, and didn't I take a truck driver and make him famous at it?"

"Yes," says Eve. "And then he went back to the trucking business, because he wasn't born an artist and the whole thing seemed silly to him. He couldn't stand the make-believe any longer, because he had no imagination, no art—nothing but the stupid ability to make money!"

Alex sinks down in a chair and throws up his hands.

"Can you beat a woman?" he asks me.

"Not in this state," I says. "It's against the law."

"Come!" says Eve. "You boys are just in time. Carrington De Vire is down at the Palace in 'The Arctic Sunflower.' I'm crazy to see it. I think he's wonderful!"

THE END